Born in 1948, Ernesto Mallo is a published essayist, newspaper columnist, screenwriter and playwright. He is a former anti-Junta activist who was pursued by the dictatorship. *Sweet Money* is the second in a trilogy with Superintendent Lascano. The first, *Needle in a Haystack*, also published by Bitter Lemon Press, won the literary prize *Premio Clarin de Novela*.

Also available from Bitter Lemon Press
by Ernesto Mallo:

Needle in a Haystack

SWEET MONEY

Ernesto Mallo

Translated by Katherine Silver

BITTER LEMON PRESS
LONDON

BITTER LEMON PRESS

First published in the United Kingdom in 2011 by
Bitter Lemon Press, 37 Arundel Gardens, London W11 2LW

www.bitterlemonpress.com

First published in Spanish as *Delincuente argentino*
by Grupo Editorial Planeta, Buenos Aires, 2007

Bitter Lemon Press gratefully acknowledges the financial
assistance of the Arts Council of England

© Ernesto Mallo, 2007
© Grupo Editorial Planeta, Buenos Aires, 2007
English translation © Katherine Silver, 2011

A CIP record for this book is available from the British Library
ISBN 978–1–904738–73–2

Typeset by Alma Books Ltd
Printed and bound by Cox & Wyman Ltd, Reading, Berkshire

The island of memory will rupture.
And life will become an artless act.
A prison for days gone by.
Tomorrow the monsters of the forest will smash
the beach upon the glass of mystery.
Tomorrow the unknown letter
will meet the hands of the soul.

Alejandra Pizarnik

1

Miranda, get your stuff!

Mole is sitting on the cot that won't be his much longer,
waiting to hear those words he's dreamt about every single one of the one thousand four hundred and sixty-one
nights he's spent in that cell block. Now that the moment
has arrived it feels unreal, and he's afraid. Inside, you
know when you've got to be on guard, when you might
be attacked. Outside, you never know where it might be
coming from, or what might go wrong. Chance is a bank
robber's worst enemy.

An air of mourning hangs over the Devoto Prison cell
block. It's always like that when a popular prisoner is
released – wonderful, yes, but, on this side of the bars,
not as cheerful as one might imagine. Prison promotes
criminal behaviour, but it also leaves you numb. The
same routine, day in and day out, slows down the re-
flexes, clouds the understanding, and, at the same time,
provokes anger. Experienced criminals know how risky
it is to go right back into action. It's all too common for
an ex-con to end up dead shortly after getting out.

Mole is a rich inmate. He is guaranteed a supply of goods and money from the outside. If you've got money, you can get virtually anything you need in prison. Miranda knows how to mete out his generosity; he shares his wealth only with the cell block's leader, The Prick. He lets him carry out the distribution however he sees fit and take credit for it. Everyone knows where the goods are coming from, but Mole would never tell. Discretion is a cardinal virtue among prisoners. That's how you garner respect. The Prick protects him and lets him have his very own prison bitch. If you've got a little smarts and you command a lot of respect, you can stay out of trouble, mostly. Anyway, riots are the most dangerous. That's when anything can happen, but the chances of getting killed during a riot are probably not much different from those of getting run over by a bus or having a flowerpot fall on your head.

In a few short minutes those words will echo down the corridor: *Miranda, get your stuff!* Then he will begin the four hundred-yard trek that separates him from the street. He'll stand up, pick up his bag – already packed – and walk down the aisle between the two rows of beds, without looking at or talking to anybody. Whatever he's not taking with him has already been given away: this is the legacy he leaves. A few hours earlier he said goodbye to everyone he had to say goodbye to. Since then, he's been slowly turning into a ghost. When you leave, you become the object of envy; when you walk out that door, you are the embodiment of everyone's desire. That's why you don't leave the goodbyes till the last moment.

In the bed next to his, Andrés, who's been his bitch for a while, is lying face down, stifling the cries that press

8

on his throat like a tie tied too tightly around his neck. Andrés loves Mole, but the sorrow he feels is not only of lost love. Miranda was good and generous to him, he always treated him considerately, he never hit him or gave him to others. A lot of guys on the block want him, but nobody ever dared. He's a green-eyed blond from Corrientes province, a guy who looks a lot like a girl. He's got all the mannerisms of a young lady, he cooks like a dream and he refers to himself as a "she" in a sweet Guarani accent. He's been inside since he was eighteen. His mother died when he was eleven, and the guy who claimed to be his father started taking advantage of him right away. One night, while the man was sleeping, Andrés tied his arms and legs to the bedposts and woke him up. He cut his penis off at the base and sat there watching him bleed to death. Then he turned himself in to the cops. At the trial, his lawyer – appointed by the court to defend the poor and the dispossessed – was too poor and too dispossessed and took the easy way out: he had him sign a confession, dictated to and written down with a large dose of animosity by the faggot-hating clerk at the police station. Nor did he bother to appeal the verdict that found Andrés guilty of first-degree murder or the sentence of life imprisonment. Miranda bought him from someone named Villar. After the transaction, Miranda made sure – without anybody finding out – that the seller got moved to a different block, just in case. A little later Villar got sick and died. Word had it that pancreatic cancer did him in.

Now Andrés is crying silently. He knows that as soon as Mole walks out that door, there will be a struggle over who gets him next. Two or three candidates are in the running, none of whom he likes. The future holds grief and suffering. Miranda tried to get involved, but The Prick advised him to keep his own counsel, to let things take their own course. He's not a man to ignore good advice and, anyway: *Who wants trouble when you're about to get out, right?* They said goodbye in a hidden corner of the prison yard. For the first and only time, Miranda let Andrés kiss him quickly on the lips… *But no tongue action, okay…* and that was the only time Andrés said to him: *I love you and I'm going to miss you. Aw, man, don't go there.* Miranda patted him on his head as if he were forgiving a naughty little boy then turned his back on him. Andrés stood there for a long time watching him through the bars. Andrés's whole body was shaking, anticipating his absence. The night before is always worse than the execution, dying much worse than death.

Miranda, get your stuff!

He stands up. He walks down the aisle between the beds, as dignified as a king and without looking at anybody, as if leaving were the most natural thing in the world. Everybody in the block stops what they're doing to watch him. Only when the door closes behind him does The Prick's powerful voice ring out in warning from the depths of the cell block.

I don't want to see you back here. You hear me, Mole?

Miranda turns around and, even though he doesn't believe in God, he gives him a sad smile and mumbles, *God willing.*

The Prick thinks he'd rather welcome him back than hear he was dead, and then it occurs to him that this thought might be a bad omen, but he doesn't want to think much about it. Fate is fate, and everybody has his own to face.

The street greets him with a blast of cold air. Nobody's there to meet him. No matter how much Susana – Duchess to him – insisted, he refused to tell her what day he was getting out. He'd also forbidden his lawyer from telling her. He'd only let her come once a month, a visit she never failed to pay and he never agreed to make more frequent. He liked her to be there, but it hurt when she left. Duchess is a good woman, and she's a looker. Miranda thinks she deserves somebody better than him.

Before seeing her, he wants to find out three things: if he has AIDS, if he can still make it with a woman, and if Susana has somebody else. Any one of these circumstances would make it impossible for him to remake his life the way he'd dreamt it. AIDS would be the most definitive but also the easiest to find out about – his friend Dr Gelser would tell him how. About making it with a woman, that's also an easy fix. Her name is Lía.

As he drives away from Bermúdez Street in the taxi he checks off his fears, one by one. Andrés promised he was healthy, and this was backed up by the fact that inmates with AIDS are put in a separate block, but you never really know. Villar's sudden death had him wondering. *If I test positive, nothing else makes any sense.* If the test turns out negative, he'll try with Lía. He's afraid a woman won't turn him on any more. Truth is, at first

11

it was a question of habit, of satisfying his need to stick his flesh into another person's body, but he'd surprised himself lately fantasizing about the night, about Andrés, about his fantastic blow jobs, about his body. He'd also started dreaming about his eyes, and that's what had him most worried. Once he's had the test he can deal with the third problem, Duchess, and find out if she has another man. The idea doesn't make him mad – he'll understand, he'll have to understand – but the pain just might kill him. He feels the need to know the truth, and he doesn't want to hear it from anybody else; he wants to see it with his own eyes. For a few days, he'll watch her every move. He'll hide near her house and find out everything. He'll hide as only he knows how to hide.

He was the champion in his neighbourhood. None of the other kids could ever find him. When they played hide-and-seek it was like he'd been swallowed up by the earth; that's how he got his nickname, Mole. His natural ability to blend into the landscape, that chameleonic talent he was born with, had served him well his entire criminal career. He had cultivated it and perfected it throughout his life, and many times it had saved him when the police had him surrounded. Very few people know that hiding is a skill that can be honed, that has rules and laws. If you want to hide effectively, the first thing you've got to do is ask yourself what your pursuer is looking for. A particular shape, a guy who's so tall or so short, who weighs so much, has a certain colour hair, is fat or skinny, has a moustache or big ears, is dressed this way or that. Whatever. The pursuer's eyes will quickly sort through everything they see, selecting anything resembling the image of the person they're looking for that he has in his head.

Miranda liked to watch documentaries about animals with his son when he was a little boy. Scientists who studied frigate birds observed that the chicks automatically opened their beaks when the mother approached to feed them. They believed this was due to the chicks' detection of their mother's shape and colour. So they did an experiment to find out if the chicks would respond to only shape and colour. They made a doll that looked like the bird, they painted it black and placed a circle of red on its chest, just like the adult females. When they saw it, the chicks opened their beaks. The researchers kept simplifying the doll until it was nothing more than a black cardboard triangle with a red mark. The chicks kept responding in the same way. Shape and colour. That's what they look for, what they recognize. The more urgent and intense the hunt and the more individuals that have to be evaluated, the fewer details get considered, and the image of the individual they're pursuing gets pared down to a few outstanding features. The quicker and more complex the hunt, the less detailed the image. Mole always knew that, instinctively. As the years passed, and thanks to his observational skills, he elevated the practice of hiding to an art form, the art of completely changing his appearance with clothes, movements, body language. He is an actor who can look eighteen years old or seventy from one minute to the next; he's the king of disguise. He also has certain innate characteristics that help: he is of average height and weight, and his face lacks any distinguishing features; it's the face of any man, every man. His hair is straight and

13

manageable, he can style it any way he wants. Only his eyes are distinctive, not because of their average brown colour, but because of the look in them: inquisitive, furtive, focused, intelligent, predatory – like the eyes of a hawk. But eyes can be easily hidden behind glasses, by looking away, by lowering the lids, and by employing that extremely rare ability to lie with them.

Night is falling when he boards the train that will take him to his hideout. The station is packed. The passengers waiting on the platform silently vie for a spot next to the edge and pray that the door will open right in front of them. The train slowly enters the station, blowing its whistle. The crowd, eager to get a seat and afraid of being pushed onto the rails, nervously jostle for position. Miranda stands in the back, neither too far away nor too close. When the train stops, the race to find a seat begins. Those closest to the doors rush headlong into the train; those further away climb in through the open windows. The second row of passengers push the first. In the third row are the old people, the pregnant women, the mothers with small children, the weak, the disabled, those who no longer want to fight. Miranda heads for the freight car. He gets in behind a group of punks dressed up for a party.

2

His chest hurts less this morning. Venancio Ismael Lascano, Perro Lascano, is wondering… Who's my protector? Who rescued me when I was lying in the street, dying, with a nine-millimetre bullet lodged between my ribs that busted my lung, already destroyed by cigarettes? What's more, his saviour had made arrangements for him to be taken care of, for medical treatment, and for rehabilitation. He set him up in this house, with a nurse, and two boring, silent guards. How long has it been? He doesn't know for sure. When he told Ramona that he was sick of being so isolated, she said that was a sign that he was recovering. Then he heard her talking on the phone in the next room, and later she announced the imminent arrival of his benefactor. That's what he's waiting for while he's thinking about Eva. Where could she be, what could have happened to her? He looks out the window. A car drives down the dirt road and past the grove of eucalyptus trees, leaving a dense trail of dust in its wake. The weather has been unusually dry the last few days. The Ford Falcon stops in front of the gate, someone gets out, opens it, waits for the car to drive through, closes it then walks slowly toward the house, a standard-issue police gun bulging under his jacket. The

15

car pulls up next to the worn-out hammock, its back door opens, and lo and behold, who should get out but Chief Inspector Jorge Turcheli, commonly known as "Blue Dollar", because even the biggest fool in town knows he's counterfeit.

To Lascano, this is quite a surprise; Turcheli is his antithesis, a corrupt policeman who got rich by making a business out of assigning precincts; cops, after all, have their preferences. The man dresses like a dandy and always looks tanned and fit. As he starts walking toward the house he sees Perro at the window, smiles and waves. Lascano doesn't respond to either the wave or the smile, he just turns to face the door Turcheli's about to enter. He thinks how good a cigarette would feel at that moment, but the doctor, who comes to check on him periodically, told him he's got to kiss cigarettes goodbye, forever. Turcheli opens the door and walks in, smiling like a diplomat.

How're you feeling? I'm intrigued, Jorge, very intrigued. What cruel doubt assails you? I don't know, first you hand me over to Giribaldi on a silver platter, then you save my life and hire a bunch of people to protect me and take care of me. A bit difficult to wrap my head around. Hey, I didn't hand you over to anybody, on the contrary, I placed you face-to-face with Giribaldi to give you a chance to get out of the mess you'd gotten yourself into. Ah, I see I have more than one reason to thank you. You've got nothing to thank me for. If you think I'm doing any of this out of the goodness of my heart, you've got another thing coming. Tell me something, how did you know where Giribaldi's men were going to hit me? I didn't know anything, you just got very lucky. Oh, really? Just when the shootout starts in Tribunales and you hit two of Giribaldi's men. A squad car gets there and calls an ambulance, because you're still breathing. Pure chance the guy on dispatch is my nephew, you know him. Who's your nephew? That Recalde kid. You don't say. Right then they call me on the radio and tell me you've been shot and you're fading fast. I tell them to take you to the police hospital. I go there and arrange things with the director, a friend of mine, tell him to make sure they take good care of you and put you in a private room. I spread the word that they killed you, and that's what I tell that dimwit Giribaldi, who swallows it whole and doesn't even check for bones. And the girl? What girl? Eva, she was with me. Don't know anything about her. Tell me, if it's not out of the goodness of your heart, why are you doing this? I'm no use to you. You're wrong there, Perro, you see, if everyone was like me we'd be totally fucked. The police force is a wonderful business opportunity, but in order for it to stay like that it's got to be minimally effective, it's got to be for real. Some of the guys don't get that, they don't realize how important that is. They don't get it that they've got to let cops like you do your job. Now, we've also got to make sure the likes of you don't get too powerful and throw a spanner in the works with your ideals. You know how Ford defined an idealist? Sounds like you're going to tell me. An idealist is a man who helps another man get rich. And the other man, what is he, a cynic? Could be, but let's not get moralistic. As I was saying, there were those who wanted to get you out of the way, not just Giribaldi and the military, in the police, too. That's why it's better for you to stay "dead", that is, if you don't want to be for real.

Turcheli stands up, looks out the window, walks over to the door, closes it and returns with a triumphant smile.

I'm going to tell you a secret. I'm listening. I've bagged the Chief of Police job. How'd you manage that? Last year I joined the sect. What sect? There's these retreats, see, they're called Christian Training Courses. All the military bigwigs, they've all been to one. It's like this. Twelve guys get together in a convent for three days. The only thing you can do is read the Bible and pray. You can't talk to anybody. Every half-hour a priest comes and gives you a lecture on God and the Devil, heaven and hell, good and bad. You know, that kind of thing. You listen and you don't say a word. That goes on for three days. I'm telling you, at a certain point your mind goes blank. And right then, as if they knew it, they start drilling your head full of that shit about the great Christian family, your obligation to help and protect one another. Anyway, that's where the guys with real power go, the generals, the admirals, the president of the chamber of commerce, the general secretary of a trade union. Imagine that. I never thought of you as religious, Jorge. It's just that if you want to rise in the world, you've got no choice. Really? No training, no promotion. Bet you can't guess who I ran into there? Carlitos Balá, the clown. Close but no cigar. Grondona. From the Football Association? No, you idiot, the other one, the TV host. You're kidding. The best part is that in the end, everyone there vows to give a hand to everyone else, always, no matter what the circumstances. A few days ago there was a big hullaballoo on TV and in the papers about a girl who was raped and killed in Belgrano. The niece of a minister, so you can imagine the uproar. I had to make some public statements. I called Grondona. Talked to his secretary. The following Sunday, there I was, on television, comforting the girl's parents, that's when I scored big points. These days, if you're not on TV, Perro, you don't exist. Real politics happens on that little screen. And this week comes my coup de grâce. We caught the guy who did it. It's all hush-hush until Thursday night. That's when I announce we've solved the case during a press conference, on TV. It's a done deal. Sunday I'm back on Grondona's programme handing the parents their daughter's killer with his hands and feet bound. You like? Not bad. And that'll do it, Perro, I'll be Chief, I'll beat the Apostles; they want it for one of their own. Who? Thin Man Filander.

When he hears that name, Perro crosses his arms and bows his head. Turcheli elaborates enthusiastically.

So, we can bring you back. Truth is, Jorge, I'm not sure I feel like returning. Just leave all that to me. I'm going to need you to keep the Apostles in their place. What makes you think I'd help you with your internal power struggles? Because you've got the soul of a cop, Perro, that's why. And because I'm better than they are.

What makes you better? First place, I saved your life; second, the Apostles are mixed up with some Turks who're mixed up with Colombian coke. They want to make Buenos Aires a transfer station to Europe. Several department higher-ups are already involved. When I become Chief, the first thing I'll do is clean that one up.

You just want to keep at your traditional business of selling precincts. You know what, Perro? It's simpler, and it's already all set up. When you get in bed with those narcos, you don't know what you're in for, those people are hell, big time. They'll take a pound of your flesh if you look at them wrong. I'm a businessman, Perro, not a man of action. With drugs, you've got to be ready for anything. I'm ambitious, but I like the good life, peace and quiet. Everything in moderation, I say, can't let yourself get too greedy.

Perro feels nauseated. He stands up and inhales deeply.

What's my status? Your file is locked away in my desk. Everyone thinks you're dead. I won't be able to keep it up for too long, but once I get my promotion, we'll set everything straight. And Giribaldi? Retired. Military officers don't even step outside in uniform any more. They've got legal problems. Things are getting rough for them. The Full Stop and Due Obedience laws they passed so we couldn't prosecute them for crimes committed during the dictatorship are full of holes. What do you mean? The kids they stole from the guerrillas, for example. Nobody can stop those trials. Because stealing a baby can't be an act of war, you understand? I understand. There's one prosecutor who's all over that, he's hunting them down, one by one, already got three or four of them behind bars.

Turcheli looks at his watch, stands up and makes ready to leave.

They tell me you're right as rain. How do you feel? Not bad. Good, let's shut down this operation, it's costing me a fortune. I've got a room for you in a pension in Palermo. Don't worry, it's not a dump. Whatever you say, but I don't have a penny. Don't worry about the dough. Ramona will take you there in a few days and she'll take care of everything. Just sit tight until I'm in, then I'll come get you. Okay? Whatever you say, but don't think for a minute that I'm going to get my hands dirty for you. We'll talk about that later.

Lascano goes over to the window to watch him leave. The dust the car kicks up is going in the other direction now. Turcheli wants to send him back to the front. His

20

life of suspended animation for his recovery and rehabilitation has come to an end. In his head, he can hear someone shout, "Action", and he knows that means the cameras are rolling once again. He has no desire to wage war against crooks and murderers, in the police force or outside of it, to be vigilant twenty-four hours a day, constantly looking over his shoulder. He has absolutely no urge to take on responsibilities, run risks. He's got nowhere to go, nowhere he wants to go, except to Eva, into her arms, her love. His close brush with death made him wiser, more detached, more calculating. He looks at the spool from which the thread of his life is unravelling, and he realizes there's not much left, and the little there is is unwinding faster and faster. He dreams of easygoing, pleasant days. He wants to lay claim to the quota of love that life has, up till now, lent him only very briefly then stolen away as if the whole thing had just been a joke. He regrets not having a picture of Eva. What he wouldn't give at this moment to look in her eyes, touch her, feel her breath, her hands. As soon as he gets back to Buenos Aires he's going to try to find out where in the world that woman is. He'll tell Jorge that he's not going to accept his proposal, and he'll ask him for money so he can find Eva. He can't imagine any other purpose or destiny, he has no interest in anything other than finding her.

As the orange sun, pierced by the thousands of eucalyptus leaves, plunges toward the horizon, Lascano's chest hurts, right where the pain of the gunshot wound mingles with that of longing.

3

The night is pitch black and it's raining. The rain is pouring down outside the windows. It's raining all over the city, the country, the world. Giribaldi is woken up by a dream he doesn't want to remember, the same one that's been waking him up for a long time. For such a long time that he's lost track. He doesn't know when he first dreamt it. Maisabé is asleep next to him and Aníbal is in the adjoining room, but he feels alone, as if there were nobody left on Earth and even these people no longer meant anything to him. He wonders if they ever did, but suspects so. The storm rattles the windowpane and an image flashes through his head, of himself jumping through it and falling in slow motion through a cloud of broken glass, just like in the movies. His fantasy dishes him up a free sample of the bolt of pain and darkness that follows his crash into the pavement; the rain falling on his mangled body mixes with his blood, then runs into the street. A few passers-by gather around his dead body and, up above, looking out from the balcony, Maisabé contemplates him, a strange smile hovering over her lips. He sits up in bed, as if he were spring-loaded. He thinks he hears a sigh. He turns to look at his wife. A line of spit dribbles out of the corner of her mouth, pulled down by the drop at the end. Steps down the hallway. The whole house creaks and whines. He hears a child cry. He enters Aníbal's room. He stands watching him for a long time. Half his face is lit by the street light shining through the window; the other half is in shadows. He's convinced the child is awake and pretending to be asleep. He walks over to him and brings his face close up to his. He's too quiet; Giribaldi wonders if he's dead. He touches him. The boy opens his eyes and stares at him without blinking. Giribaldi pulls back and looks away. He leaves the room. He goes to his office and opens the French doors onto the balcony. The raindrops bounce off the floor and splash his bare feet. He goes out onto the balcony and looks down, calculating exactly where his body would land. The rain is icy cold. He withdraws into the room. He closes the door to his office and sits down at his desk. He doesn't know what to do with the tremendous urge he has to cry. He sits there contemplating nothingness until morning comes and the household comes alive.

Maisabé brings him a cup of strong, black coffee, without sugar, puts it silently down on the desk and leaves. At the exact instant she vanishes from his sight, she says, *Good morning.* Giribaldi doesn't answer; he looks at the steaming cup; he smells the aroma of the coffee as if it were a memory. The only thing that's real is what's happening at this very moment. The minutes, the hours, the days spill into the emptiness, the endless void. He brings the cup to his lips and doesn't realize, until much later, that the liquid has burnt his tongue. He wonders if his numbness is due to a terminal illness.

He waits for more than three hours before the secretary informs him that a problem has come up and the general won't be able to make it. She doesn't offer him another appointment, she says she'll consult with her boss and call him. Her voice lacks conviction, her words are half-hearted, she makes not the slightest effort to pretend. Major (Ret.) Leonardo Giribaldi leaves the building at 250 Azopardo and starts walking toward Corrientes. He, like so many other military officers who were discharged when Alfonsín promoted more modern ones, has become a pariah. Nobody is going to stick his neck out for them or defend them. On top of that, it seems they should now be grateful that they're not being put on trial. The worst part is that nobody tells them what's going on, everybody simply ignores them, as if they had never existed.

Giribaldi is trembling with rage. He sits down on a bench in the plaza and tries to calm down. From high atop a pillar, Columbus looks toward Spain, his back to the Casa Rosada, the presidential palace. A palace that's never occupied, he believes, by great men, patriots, those who devote their lives to serving their country. The blue-and-white flag waves from over one of the balconies. During other eras, its majestic flutter filled him with pride; now all he feels is shame. The communists managed to take over. What they couldn't win as men, on the battlefield, they won by seducing the people, who always want to be flattered. He looks at the window of the office of the President of Argentina.

I bet that's where he is, that fat faggot bastard, that traitor. He got rid of the entire general staff. Passed a bunch of useless laws. Made us think that the only ones who'd be put on trial for actions against the guerrillas would be the top commanders, the members of the Junta. But when it was their turn to sit in the dock, they opened their big traps and said they didn't know what was going on. How could they possibly not have known!? The ones who have taken their places dress up in the costume of democracy, as if they didn't have anything to do with it either. They just sat around on their big fat asses praying every night that they wouldn't come for them, and they played their cards very carefully. And here we are, the ones who did all the work, the ones out on the front lines risking our lives, now it's our lives on the line.

He tries to push these thoughts away because they make him feel like he's going to explode with rage. He's got to do something, get busy, or he's afraid he'll go crazy. He gets up, spits on the gravel path and turns toward the post office. It's time for the stampede of office workers. Tomorrow he has an appointment with Gutiérrez, who made a lot of dough as commander of a task force and used it to start a cleaning and security business. Seems he's doing well, but when they spoke he told him, *As long as you don't get your hopes up, come on over and we'll have a cup of coffee.* He already knows he's not going to give him a job, but at least they can talk. For too long his wife has been practically the only person he talks to. All Maisabé goes on about is the house, the boy's school, the prices, the money that's never enough.

He walks down the stairs into the subway along with a rushing, chaotic and undisciplined crowd. All these noisy, disorderly people make him sick. He represses an urge to bark out an order for them all to fall into line.

If he had the slightest hope of being obeyed, Giribaldi would divide them into two groups: those going up and those going down. Those boarding the train would take one step back to leave room for those getting off. Once the cars were emptied out in an orderly fashion, the others could step forward and enter. Quick, efficient, organized, clean. This upsets him – people on the loose, struggling for space, pushing each other like animals in a corral. If it were in his power he would impose rational discipline that would save them from their own bestiality, this promiscuous rubbing of body against body, this total lack of respect for each other's space. But he has no power at all. Once he did, and he could exercise that power anywhere and everywhere and at any time. Then his power was limited to the barracks. Now: nothing.

While he waits for the train, whose slow and tentative headlights are already shining through the tunnel, he feels like anybody, like nobody, like one more victim of the shoves and neglect of these civilians, civilians who are utterly oblivious to the debt of gratitude they owe men like him. People crowd around, get tenser and tenser, preparing for their attack on the seats. Giribaldi, a bit stupefied from staring at the lights that grow as they approach, thinks about the minuscule distance that separates him from death: one step and it's over. Everything. Someone touches his back. His first thought is that they want to push him onto the tracks. He wheels around, his hand flying to the nine-millimetre gun in his shoulder holster, and he glues a furious eye onto a young yuppie. He looks him over – a two-day stubble, black suit, yellow tie and colourful backpack. The yuppie doesn't even look back at Giribaldi, he's in his own world, his ears covered by earphones echoing a rhythmic *dum-dum* that keeps time with the swaying of his head. The crowd starts to move and, with the force of a wave, sweeps Giribaldi into the train.

4

Marcelo moved out of his parents' house less than four months ago. Now only his mother's, because Mario passed on a week after Marcelo moved out. That death was anticipated, though not expected so soon. There were unexpected complications due to bronchitis, the doctors made the diagnosis and the old man came down with acute septicaemia. A few days earlier, when Marcelo asked him how he was, he delivered his last good line: *Well, truth is, I'm much closer to the harp than the guitar.* He died from one day to the next. Marcelo has dinner with his mother two or three times a week.

Due to the customary period of mourning, he had to delay his marriage to Vanina. A few days after his father died, he was appointed Public Prosecutor. He benefited from the resignation of many judicial officials who were not keen to have their actions during the dictatorship investigated. He attributed his promotion to his father, a little help from the above and beyond. Then he felt odd for having entertained such a thought. Life after death seemed to him about as probable as a pig with wings. But it was his private way of acknowledging everything his father had given him, everything he was grateful for.

Vanina was the most beautiful girl in high school, and now she is the most beautiful girl in the architecture department at the university. Though perhaps a little too aware of her beauty, she is polite and well educated. Marcelo thinks that her self-consciousness makes her movements less spontaneous, too studied, designed to emphasize her best features of face and figure and made to please whatever – people, animals, even objects – she has in front of her. They are both still caught up in how they are seen by their group of high-school friends, a group in which they are "the" couple. She has always been quite keen on the idea of getting married and having a family, but she accepts the excuse of Mario's death to postpone the wedding with fewer protests than Marcelo would have hoped for, and more anger than he could have ever imagined. He doesn't realize that Vanina's anger smoulders away inside her like live embers, embers one notices only when they burn you. Since his appointment as a Public Prosecutor, he's had a deluge of projects he's wanted to work on. Investigations, open cases, a series of crimes committed by the military during the dictatorship that have never been brought to trial or punished, that have been bogged down in a series of laws and contradictory decrees, in many cases unconstitutional, which he would have to disentangle and pursue in opposition to the government's lack of political will to prosecute criminals in uniform.

Mama is in the kitchen putting the last touches to the meal. The room that was his is exactly the same as it was the day he left it. That his mother has left it intact feels a bit creepy, even ghoulish, like when parents of a child who has died make cenotaphs of their rooms. Marcelo came to look for something he left there when he used to be a clerk in Judge Marraco's court, documents pertaining to an investigation that was left unresolved – the Biterman case. When he takes the envelope off the bookshelf, he knocks to the floor a book by Kelsen his father gave him when he started studying law. He sits down on the bed, puts down the envelope and picks up the book. In spite of being an impenitent reader, his father didn't like writing at all, not even a dedication, but he did highlight one paragraph in yellow: *Justice, for me, is the shield under whose protection science – and along with science, truth and sincerity – can flourish. This is the justice of freedom, the justice of peace, the justice of democracy, the justice of tolerance.*

He smiles. That morning he has been working on several cases of children of the disappeared, those who were stolen by the military during the dictatorship. The Grandmothers of the Plaza de Mayo had supplied him with evidence, some of which mentioned a military base in the provinces that was used as a base of operations and clandestine detention centre, named Coti Martínez. It was believed that Coti was short for *Comando de Operaciones Tácticas I.* Several witnesses implicated a major by the name of Giribaldi. He made note of that name, which was somehow familiar. He had seen it before, and he spent all morning trying to remember exactly where. In the afternoon, while he was having lunch with Mónica, his friend and mentor, a judge in the criminal courts, suddenly, between bites of Don Luis's steak with mushroom sauce, he remembered: his name had figured in the Biterman case.

Superintendent Lascano, otherwise known as Perro, gave Marraco all the evidence related to Biterman's murder, in which Giribaldi was a suspect. The situation was as follows: as was common at that time, the task force, or death squad, commanded by the major had executed two young people, a man and a woman, in an empty field. By chance, a truck driver stopped on the shoulder to take a piss and saw the dead bodies. He drove away and reported what he'd seen at the Puente de la Noria police station. A little earlier that same night, a man named Amancio Pérez Lastra had an altercation with Elías Biterman, a money lender from the Once neighbourhood to whom he owed a lot of money. Biterman ended up dead. Pérez Lastra then turned to his old friend Giribaldi to help him dispose of the body. The major suggested he dump it in the same place where he'd shot the two subversives. In the meantime, Lascano was sent to the scene to investigate the two dead bodies the truck driver had reported, but when he arrived, he found three dead bodies, one of which exhibited many features different from the other two. Lascano realized that this corpse had been dumped there rather than executed by the military. He began investigating and all hell broke loose. He identified the murderer and the weapon used in the crime, and specified each link in the chain of complicity. Marraco did not include any of this evidence in his investigation, and Marcelo was an eyewitness to this intentional concealment of evidence. Instead, the judge instructed Marcelo to take the file to Giribaldi, which Marcelo did after he made photocopies of its contents. Those documents, which implicate Giribaldi in the death of a civilian, are in that envelope he is now holding in his hands.

Tomorrow he will try to find Lascano. He has the feeling he might be biting off more than he can chew. His mother calls him to the table. He puts all the documents back in the envelope. He decides to also take Kelsen's book with him.

The aroma wafting down the hallway makes his stomach growl like a crocodile: his mother makes the best risotto in the world.

5

Jorge shaves meticulously and for a long time. He opens the tap and contemplates with satisfaction as the bathroom fills up with steam. He undresses and steps into the very hot shower. His wife says he boils himself rather than bathes. He washes his hair with herbal shampoo, scrubs his body with scentless glycerine soap, then rinses twice. He dries himself off in front of the open window, feeling his pores closing in the cold breeze. He takes a bottle of Fahrenheit cologne out of the medicine cabinet. He aims the spray at the ceiling and lets the cloud of scent fall over his skin like a morning mist. These moments of his morning ablutions are when he plans his day, when he feels most inspired. He's quite satisfied this morning. Despite all the Apostles' manoeuvrings and the pressure they applied to secure the position for one of their own, he got it. He remembers Filander's angry look the day he was sworn in, and he smiles. Now he must quickly dismantle their operation. Those guys are no sissies, and he can't expect them to roll over and play dead. That very morning he will begin to execute his plan to decapitate the organization. He knows he doesn't have a moment to lose; he can't give them time to get a foothold, surround him, throw him off balance. In one fell swoop he will move Cubas to the Oran precinct, he'll open an internal investigation of Valli and Medina – up to their eyeballs in the racket of stripping stolen cars – and he'll put Bellón and García on administrative leave. Filander has to die. He'd rather avoid such a measure, and he resorts to it only when he has absolutely no other choice; this, he believes, is such a case. Filander is a dangerous lunatic. He trusts the rest will scurry away like cockroaches when the lights go on. Then he'll deal with them in a few days. Ladeski has had it in for Hernández ever since he got the upper hand and kept the fifteenth precinct. If he promises it to one of them and gives the seventeenth, for example, to the other, he's got a good chance of getting them both on his team. He'll first have to see their reactions, but he's almost sure they'll come on board with him. He just has to wait and see.

He goes back to the bedroom, where Cora has laid his clean clothes out on the bed. The shirt is impeccably ironed, the trousers have a crease so sharp you could cut salami with it – as his old man used to say – and the shoes are shined so brightly he could use them as mirrors to shave in. He takes a sip of maté through the *bombilla* straw as he contemplates himself in the mirror. He isn't carrying an ounce of fat, and the few grey hairs that have appeared here and there give him a touch of distinction.

I've still got my good looks.

He gives the maté back to his wife and puts on the jacket of his spanking-new Chief of Police uniform.

So, my love, are you proud of your hubbie? You know I am, Jorge. It's just that I'm worried that now I'll see even less of you than I did before. Don't you worry about a thing. I'm not worried, it's just that the kids treat this place like a hotel, coming here to eat and sleep, and you work more and more every day, and all I do is sit here alone and watch the mould grow. You've got your mother, your friends. It's not the same, Jorge, it's just not the same. What do you say we go out to eat to celebrate? Oh, I don't know, you think we should? I can't figure you out. Should I tell the kids? No, just the two of us. Oh, I don't know. I'll call you later and we'll arrange it. Whatever you say, Jorge. Would I have to get dressed? I guess, unless you want to go naked.

Graciela is waiting for him at the entrance on Moreno Street. She, too, is wearing a brand-new uniform. She greets him with a *Good morning, sir,* and a cheeky wink. They have a perfect understanding. The entire department suspects there's something going on between them. And there is, but the secret they share is very different from the one the others imagine. She follows him into his office. Jorge asks her to get him the phone numbers of a series of people whose names she writes down on her pad. She closes the door behind her, sits down at her desk and begins to look up the numbers. Jorge, sitting at his desk, is figuring out what he should do first. In front of him he has the police organizational chart, with all the names and their corresponding positions. He begins the task of moving people around. Internal Affairs: he crosses out Crio. He puts a line through Superintendent Olindo Gaito and writes in Lascano. Vice: get rid of…

In the reception room, Graciela is writing down telephone numbers next to the names Jorge dictated to her. The door opens and two superintendents she already knows, a civilian and one young female officer she's never seen enter.

You'll be leaving now. What did you say, sir? That you'll be leaving now. Where, sir? Home, you've got the day off. I'll just go tell the Chief. We'll take care of the Chief. But... No buts, just leave, now!

The man is whispering, but his tone and the look in his eyes brook no argument. Graciela grabs her purse and walks out, her chest heaving with distress. The female officer sits down in Graciela's chair behind the desk and hands the pad with the names and numbers to Superintendent Valli. He reads, smiles smugly, shows it to Bellón, tears off the sheet, stuffs it in his pocket and hands the pad back to the policewoman. He looks at the civilian.

Everything ready, Doctor? Ready. Let's go.

Valli and Bellón enter the office; the doctor follows behind and closes the door. Jorge starts to get up, but Valli is already on him, pushing him back down in the chair. Bellón stands behind Jorge and pins his arms back. Valli puts Jorge's neck in a lock with his right arm as he grabs his hair with his left. The doctor approaches, pushes open Jorge's jacket and, with both hands, rips open his shirt, tearing off the buttons. Jorge tries to move, but Bellón holds his arms and Valli has his neck. The doctor takes out of one pocket a ten centimetre-long cardiac needle and out of the other a vial of adrenaline. He places the needle in the plunger, pulls up the plastic pump, grabs the whole thing as if it were a dagger, and in one swift movement stabs it into Jorge's chest with expert precision. Jorge feels a sharp pain in his heart; he fixes his bulging eyes on the doctor, who presses on the pump, emptying the contents of the syringe into his heart muscle. Jorge has a spasm and kicks the doctor in the shin, making him swear. He throws his head back and begins to shake violently. The two superintendents have to hold him down with all their strength, his eyes fill with blood, he desperately gasps for breath, he grows stiff, then relaxes, then dies with his eyes and mouth open. The two policemen are sweating and trembling from the exertion. The doctor touches his neck to feel for a pulse. Valli looks at the papers on the desk, picks up the organizational chart, reads it, folds it twice and puts it in his pocket.

Ready. Let's go.

The three men leave the office. The policewoman is in the same place they left her. Valli picks up the telephone and dials a number...

...it's done.

He hangs up.

In half an hour, you sound the alarm and call the ambulance at this number. Yes, sir. Do you have any questions about what you rehearsed? You know exactly what you are supposed to do and say? Yes. Are you okay? Yes, fine. Don't fail me. Don't worry about anything.

The men leave the reception room. The policewoman accompanies them to the door and locks it behind them. She walks to the office. She enters. She goes up to Jorge's body and touches his neck to look for a pulse. She leaves. She wipes off the two doorknobs with a handkerchief, closes the office door, unlocks the door to the reception area and sits down in front of the desk. She looks at her watch and sighs.

The whole thing took less than three minutes.

6

Miranda spends the whole night as if he'd been bitten by a tsetse fly: tossing and turning, floating in a vague half-sleep, falling into a deeper sleep for mere minutes, maybe seconds, at a time. He spends his first night of freedom full of regrets, fears, guilt and the constant urge to cry. He is tormented as only a tough man, hardened and moulded by life's harsh realities can be when all his defences fall away; he feels like a slug starting down a path strewn with salt. Even his pores feel sorrow and ache. He is overwhelmed by a sense of vertigo, and the only escape appears to be the end of this interminable night. Tomorrow he will confront his greatest fear, hear his final sentence. He knows this is one of those all-or-nothing moments he has had to confront several times throughout his life. There have been times he's even gone looking for them and then boasted about surviving them. But now he's weary, he wants it to stop. He cannot imagine life as an invalid, or without his woman or his son. He gets up, goes to the bathroom and looks at himself in the mirror, where all the marks stamped on his face by the prison bars are reflected back at him, no detail spared: his left eye slightly crossed – which wasn't like that before – the brown spot on his temple, his receding gums that now expose the tips of the roots of his teeth –

which themselves have yellowed. He is sick of that insipid face staring heartlessly back at him. He hates mirrors. Now that they've let him out of his cage he can allow himself this moment of tremendous weakness, which anyway was inevitable. He feels sorry for himself and hates himself for feeling that way. He despises the man he has always been, the one he no longer wants to be, the man who is determined to change, come what may.

The black of the sky edges toward blue, then continues to lighten. The arrival of what Miranda waited for all night does not lift his spirits. Lying in the bathtub with his eyes closed and abandoning himself to the warmth of the water enveloping him, he thinks: *This is the ideal way: a razor blade in the bathtub. Uncork the blood, fall asleep, let it flow like water. Leave his wife and son a pale, clean corpse, as if he were sleeping. Nothing pathetic, sordid or bloody. Something that can be buried with decorum.*

Doctor Gelser had to twice postpone his appointment with Peretti because the entryway was swarming with police. He is a prudent man and doesn't want to run the risk of someone recognizing him and starting to ask questions. But at that moment, the entrance to Churruca Police Hospital is particularly peaceful. He looks at his watch. He walks from the corner with quick steps. He's wearing a doctor's white coat. As he enters, he keeps his head down, past the elevators and directly to the door that leads to the basement. The corridor is empty. He stops in front of the supply window and rings the bell. It opens briefly, then shuts with a bang. Gelser walks over to the door next to the window; Peretti, a big guy wearing blue overalls, appears.

Come in, Sawbones.

Gelser enters. Peretti looks up and down the corridor and closes the door. He takes a box off a shelf and gives it to him.

Here's your order. Great. As long as I'm here, I need something else. If I've got it, it's yours. A Finocchietto rib-splitter. Wait a second...

Peretti picks up a styrofoam box and places it on the table in front of Gelser.

Anything else? That's all for now. Did you work something out with the people in the pharmacy? We'll have to wait till next week when the Turk comes back from vacation; that jerk who took his place would be better lost than found. Okay. Let me know if you need anything. You know I will, Sawbones.

Gelser takes out a small wad of banknotes held together with a rubber band and stuffs them into one of Peretti's pockets.

That's for the order, what do I owe you for the rib-splitter? It's on the house, Sawbones. Really? Natch. Thanks a million.

Peretti picks up the telephone and dials three numbers.

Wait for me to clear your way... Vasco?... Sawbones Gelser is on his way out with some merchandise. Make sure the coast is clear for him... Okay... They're really breaking people's balls on the way out. Thanks, we'll be in touch. You're welcome, any time.

43

It's almost eleven in the morning by the time Mole leaves his hideout. The morning has dished him up a perfectly splendid autumn day. The sun: perfect; the temperature: perfect, even exhilarating. He walks to Gelser's house. Where that is, exactly, is one of the best kept secrets in the criminal underworld. Nobody would dare even mention that it exists, no matter how tight a spot they're in. It's where fugitives go to get treatment when they've been wounded by officers of the law or rival criminals, which are often one and the same.

Sawbones used to practise medicine in the poor neighbourhood of Claypole, where he'd been born and raised. One night the local police superintendent asked him to perform an abortion on a minor, but the pregnancy was too far along and he refused. They framed him and threw the book at him. In the end, he lost his licence and became the doctor of the underworld. He's a genius at removing bullets, a true master at preventing and curing infections. If there's dough, he charges; if not, no problem. He never leaves anybody out in the cold. The doctor has earned himself a place of respect, gratitude and appreciation, even among the most violent and crazy lowlifes.

There's no lock on the door, but inside are all the trappings of a regular doctor's office, even a small operating room equipped with everything he managed to rescue from his former practice, as well as what Peretti supplies him. Gelser comes out to greet him, flashing his magnificent smile.

My dear, dear Mole, what a pleasure, come in, come in. When did you get out? Yesterday. Everything okay? Well, you know what it's like, those first hours out. Terrifying. Look, I know someone, a psychoanalyst, he was inside and now he does therapy for ex-cons. Are you interested? Hey, man, if we've got psychoanalysts for cons, you know we're lost. So leave me alone with that crap. That's all I need. So, what do you need? Look... I want you to test me for the plague. The ELISA test, for HIV? For AIDS. Right, that's for HIV. What do I have to do? It's nothing. Go to this address. Ask to speak to Alberto, tell him I sent you. Here's the lab order. You won't have to pay anything. Money's not a problem. It's on me. You'll have the results in two days. Let me take a look at you. Take off your shirt.

Gelser stands up and looks in his eyes with a little device that emits a very bright white light, then in his throat and ears, listens to his chest through a stethoscope and palpates his lymph nodes.

You look as healthy as a horse to me. But you want to be sure, right? Yeah, of course. I want to get back with Duchess, but not if I've got it. How many were you with inside? Just one. The whole time? No, in the last year. Was he with anybody else? Just me. That's good.

After he leaves the laboratory Miranda calls Screw and they arrange to meet that evening at Topolino, a pizzeria in downtown Haedo, in the suburbs of Buenos Aires. Screw is the one who manages Mole's money. While Mole was in jail, he made sure he and his family had whatever they needed. He has carried out his duty with remarkable loyalty and meticulousness, he has accounted

45

forevery penny and gives many more explanations than Miranda demands. They agree to meet at ten that night.

Mole arrives first and orders a large, half-mozzarella, half-onion with cheese pizza and a beer. Screw shows up one minute later. Miranda watches him step around two barefoot kids asking for spare change in the street in front and enter quickly; he stands up and gives him a hug and a kiss on the cheek. He's truly happy to see him, but Screw looks distraught.

What's up, old man, why the long face? You're going to kill me. What's going on? It's all gone, Mole, I've lost almost all your dough. What do you mean lost? I didn't want to tell you because I hoped I'd get it back before you got out, but I couldn't.

With great solemnity, and racked with shame, Screw places an envelope on the table. Miranda stares at it, unable to get over the shock.

What's this? It's all that's left.

Mole peeks in the envelope and casts a disappointed eye on the bundle of dollars inside, then puts it in the inside pocket of his jacket.

But what happened? My baby girl is sick.

Screw's eyes fill with tears. He lowers his head. The waiter places the wooden platter with the pizza on the table, opens the Quilmes beer and walks away. Mole pours out the beer and hands Screw a glass. Screw finishes it in one gulp. He looks up from the foam in the glass and meets Mole's eyes. His face is twisted with grief. His voice sounds like his tongue is a wet rag.

She's dying, Mole.

He looks down and burps. Miranda calls over the waiter.

Do me a favour, kid. Put the pizza in a box and give it to those kids out front. Seems we've lost our appetite.

Mole stares silently at his friend, then pulls himself together.

You're going to kill me. Stop talking crap, will you? What do you mean, I'm going to kill you? I would if I were you. Nothing can be done? I spent all the dough on tests to see what she had. And? It's a brain tumour. Inoperable, no treatment. All I can do is sit around and watch her die. She's blind...

Miranda, seeing that Screw's about to fall apart again, squeezes his arm to bring him around. He doesn't want to hear any more about it. He has no room for his friend's pain. Prison has left him with dead zones that will take a long time to come back to life.

It's okay, Screw, calm down. What can I do? You had to spend it, and you spent it on a good cause. The problem is, you didn't let me know. 'Cause you know what, buddy, when you hear news like that your blood pressure goes up. You can't think clearly and you don't know what to do. Of course, I understand you... No, Mole, I'm sorry, but you don't understand. Nobody who

47

*hasn't gone through this can understand. Your head explodes.
Nothing that mattered to you matters any more. Nothing makes
sense any more. You feel totally alone, totally abandoned. All
you can do is watch yourself suffer as you watch the disease
consuming your daughter's life and see that empty look in the
doctors' eyes that says that they don't know anything, either,
that there's nothing they can do. Even what I'm telling you now
doesn't really get at it, Mole. I can't find the words to tell you
what I'm going through.*

Suddenly his friend is out of reach. All Mole can do is
look at him: Screw brings his hand to his forehead, drops
his head again and a sigh comes out of his mouth that
sounds like a muffled howl, almost inaudible, but that
makes Miranda's bones twinge as if someone had used
a cattle prod on him.

*As soon as I can I'll get it back to you, Mole, I promise. Do me
a favour and cut the crap about the dough, Screw. Okay, Mole,
thank you. Yeah, cut the crap. I gotta go. Take it easy.*

Miranda stands up to give his friend a hug, but Screw
avoids it, holds out his hand in a brief moment of des-
peration, then leaves without looking back. Mole watches
him through the window as he turns the corner and
disappears into the night. He finishes the beer in three
gulps, pays and leaves. It's cold outside.

He starts walking. This is one thing he never expected.
Screw's miserable face has remained stamped on his
retina like a curse. And what if tomorrow the test comes
out bad, and it turns out he's condemned like Screw's
daughter? What would he do if something like that

48

happened to his son? He pushes that thought away with a grunt. He can't even conceive of it. Miranda is capable of facing anything, rising to any occasion, but he doesn't do well with problems he can't do anything to fix, situations where the only possible course of action is no action, merely acceptance. Acceptance is an art that nobody would dream of practising voluntarily. It's always imposed on us by the most implacable of tyrants: Mother Nature. The closest Miranda has ever come is resignation, which he's practised every time human justice has placed him behind bars. But resignation is temporary, and even while it lasts, you can always do something, plan something, think about a future or find a crack – doing yourself in? – to escape through. But acceptance is reserved for when there is absolutely no other option, when it's the only choice left.

He follows the same route he saw Screw take as he watched him through the window. Miranda watched him – alone, divorced from the world by a tragedy that places him out of reach of any comfort – knowing that he couldn't do anything for his friend, that nobody could. But he has to do something for himself. He has very little money left. Soon it'll be completely gone. He walks until his legs hurt, then he goes to his hideout and lies down, fully dressed, on the bed.

The La Plata train station looks just like it did when he first saw it as a child. He's on the platform looking through a window at Duchess and Fernando, his son, sitting in the waiting room. Suddenly the train whistle blows, the engine spews out a blast of steam, and it starts to move. But it's not the train that's moving, it's the station. It's not his wife and son who leave; it's the station, it's him. That image continues to cause him indescribable anguish for a long time after he's already woken up.

7

Give me more morphine. Let's see... what time is it? No, not yet, you'll have to wait a few more hours. Why? We've got to save it for the night, when the pain gets much worse. So, give me some now, and again at night. No way. What, are you worried about me getting addicted? It's a possibility, but what I'm really afraid of is that you won't have the opportunity. It's a wonderful drug, but the price is high and the bill comes due fast. If your blood pressure drops too much I won't be able to do anything. Do you have any idea how much this hurts? No, I've never been shot. I wouldn't wish it on you, I feel like I'm being torn apart at the seams. Listen, there're many ways to deal with pain, and the way you're dealing with it is the worst. Oh yeah, how's that? You're resisting it. What should I do? Relax, enjoy it. What the hell are you talking about? I'm not a masochist. That's not what I'm talking about. What are you talking about? Have you ever stopped to think about the purpose of pain? To fuck up your life? No, to save it. If there were no pain, you wouldn't realize you'd been shot, for example, and you'd bleed to death quite cheerfully. You're right. Pain is the language your body uses to tell your brain that something's wrong, where it's wrong and how serious it is. I understand, but it could use gentler words. Pain is a force of nature, and nature doesn't let its creatures ignore it when it has something to say. You can't argue with nature. So? So, pain is a signal. And? When you resist it or try to ignore it, it's not doing its job, and it will keep trying. Which means? Which means it will keep hurting. On the other hand, if you pay attention, it will have carried out its mission and will let up a little. If it were that simple we wouldn't need painkillers. Painkillers block your perception of the pain for a short time, so you can rest. They help. Especially for men who are such wimps about pain. Are you calling me a wimp? All men are a bit wimpy about pain; if they ever gave birth they'd know what pain was. You can't compare. What? Giving birth and getting shot. Okay, I won't compare. Anyway, this business of you calling me a wimp, you're just taking advantage of me because I'm wounded. If I wanted to take advantage of you, I wouldn't give a damn about your wound.

Just as the last words are leaving her mouth, Ramona turns her back on him, picks up the tea tray and walks toward the house. Lascano watches her. Her straight black hair dances to the cadence of her walk. He wonders how it would feel sliding down his belly. Desire shines in his eyes, which she can no longer see, desire she guessed at long before Lascano even had a clue he felt it. She reminds him of Eva.

As fleeting as their meeting was, it has left its mark on him, as only true love can. Before Eva, there was Marisa, the woman he loved without a shadow of a doubt and who abandoned him forever when she died, just when he loved her more than ever. His grief lasted until he met Eva, who looked so much like Marisa that it was like she had come back for act two. With Marisa's death, he'd lost all hope of ever finding love, he'd become some kind of ascetic who could only be aroused by memory or fantasy.

Eva erupted into his life with the power of a gale-force wind or, as Ramona would put it, like a force of nature. With her animal love, she reinfected him with the virus of desire. The indisputable urge for a woman's body. She reminded him that his physical being was subject to the imperatives of the species, imperatives that demand, for moments of dazzling urgency, that this thing hanging between his legs be inserted into one precise spot, that it has a purpose it must carry out. Men disguise this urge to conquer, equate it with the hunting of prey, think we're in charge when we are really just submitting to the imperatives of reproduction. Not to mention that the best part of the hunt is really when we are being hunted.

The afternoon sun falls slowly behind the eucalyptus trees. The leaves quiver. Friday's first star makes its appearance in the dark sky. Lascano hears the sound of the screen door opening, Ramona's steps on the quartzite path set with shells. The breeze carries her perfume ahead of her, announcing her arrival.

Time to go inside. Will you give me a hand? That's what I'm here for.

Lascano no longer needs help getting up. They both know that, but Ramona leans down so he can put his arm around her shoulders. She holds him around the waist and helps him stand up. Once on his feet, he closes his eyes to better feel this woman's proximity. In his mind he inevitably makes comparisons. Where he expects to find a curve, there's bone; where his hand predicts hair, there's smoothness. His touch remembers, longs

53

for another body. There's something false about this closeness. His reservations are fleeting, the unexpected makes way for curiosity.

I'm not so sure you still need help. You have no idea how much I do.

When they get to the bedroom, he sits down on the bed; she stands there looking at him. He doesn't have the patience for insinuations. Just as he's about to speak, she places her finger on his lips. She goes and switches off the light, walks to the window, opens it and pulls open the shades. A powerful scent of jasmine wafts into the room. Ramona sits down next to him. Lascano lets himself collapse, his head coming to rest on her lap, then looks up at her. The rest of the world is in suspense. She is staring off at the leaves in the garden; he can tell she is also missing someone. Perhaps she too is curious and wants to find out what there is besides this attraction. Maybe she's afraid, as he is. Then Lascano does what he must, he overcomes his fear, sits up, puts his arms around her, kisses her, touches her, undresses her, caresses her. Slowly, she joins in and starts playing the game, dancing to the music of the breath, the cadence of the blood, the piping of the flutes, the glances, the creaking of wood, the blowing of the bellows, the plucking of the strings, the pulsing, banging marimbas, vibraphones, kettledrums, which bear them aloft to the end, where she, already sated, begs him to come, for now she wants to receive his warm semen, this other semen, a final ringing of chimes, once, twice and again… the telephone, it's the telephone that keeps ringing.

Leaving Lascano alone with the aftereffects of a stupendous session of loveless sex, Ramona gets up and walks across the room naked, as majestic as the Seventh Fleet entering the Mediterranean. Lascano lies back in bed, enjoying the release of tension and the cool night air on his overheated body. The effort has left him exhausted, and the pain of his chest wound has returned, steady and implacable. From the adjacent room he hears Ramona's voice but not her words. He hears a tone of urgency, a vibration of alarm. Lascano sits up, suddenly and totally alert. When she returns, the expression on her face tells him immediately that recess is over. She quickly starts getting dressed. Fear propels her haste.

We have to get out of here. What's going on? Jorge's dead. What? You heard. How? The official story is that he had a heart attack in his office, but they think they killed him. Who? I didn't ask; what's more, I don't want to know. I'll help you get dressed. Where are we going? I don't know, we'll think of somewhere on the way. Did they tell you we were in danger? They told me we should make ourselves scarce, very scarce.

8

Miranda's gait reflects his anxiety. One part of him just wants to get it over with, wants to know already, but the other part of him is scared to death. The news about Noelia, Screw's daughter, plays over and over in his head like a stubborn melody. Then there's Andrés's eyes... and Villar's ghost, chiding him at every turn. That pink spot that appeared under his nipple. This morning his eyes were very red when he got up. Maybe it's the price you pay, he thinks, for a year of buggering a dude, and so much for his excuse that's it was just for survival, for the release he needed. Maybe he should have been stoical and made do only with masturbating.

He walks through the lobby of the laboratory. When the elevator doors open he finds himself face-to-face with a guy who's got death tattooed all over him. His dim, sunken eyes seem to be interrogating him. Miranda steps aside at the same moment and in the same direction as the sick man. The action repeats itself until finally they coordinate and each one goes on his way. He no longer has any doubts: this encounter has confirmed his worst fears that he is doomed. Now nothing will have any meaning. His dearth of funds, Noelia's illness, Duchess and her supposed lovers. In this case, he thinks, everything will boil down to one simple question: should he slash his wrists with a razor blade? As he walks up to the counter where they give out the test results, he thinks about his own funeral and the image of his son standing next to his coffin makes his throat constrict. The beautiful young woman in white attends efficiently to those waiting in line to pick up the results of their tests. When it's his turn, Miranda feels like his heart is about to explode. The girl hands him the envelope and notices how his hand is shaking. She looks him in the eye and offers him a splendid smile:

No need to worry, sir, if it was positive the doctor would have given it to you personally.

Miranda has a moment of surprise before feeling like the biggest idiot on the planet. But what really pisses him off is that this divine young thing has just called him *sir*. He's a new man when he re-emerges on the street and tears open the envelope: Antibodies ANTI-HIV1/ HIV2… Negative (ELISA). He crumples up the piece of paper and throws it in a trash can. It's a sunny morning and life itself is singing through the streets.

He spends the rest of the day re-establishing contacts, digging around, finding out what people are up to. Who lost, who died, who's bolted, what's in the works, and what's up with the Federal Police, dubbed by themselves in typically modest Argentinean fashion as "the best in the world". He collects information here and there, patiently gathering facts and more facts, by telephone and in the cafés where the denizens of his world hang out. The panorama starts to take shape in his head, a map of the current situation and future possibilities. On the one hand, he's angry. For a long time he'd been mulling over the idea of fundamentally changing his life, of starting a legitimate business, something tranquil, of keeping out of trouble, finally giving Duchess the life she's been wanting for as long as he can remember. Settling down, becoming the family man he thinks he is deep down and welcoming his grandchildren when they come along. Maybe, just maybe, when his time is up, he'll die peacefully in his own bed. But now that he knows his money has been devoured by Noelia's illness, none of that will be possible. Not in the short run at least. He's up a blind alley, and this setback pisses him off. Again he has to resort to a bank job, but the more he thinks about it, the more the anger begins to give way to a quite different sensation. Something akin to vertigo lodges in the pit of his stomach and sends currents of electricity to his muscles, focuses his vision and lets him shake off the last traces of lethargy left over from prison. This heist, he promises himself briefly, will be the last one. It will be the heist to end all heists. Now the world ceases to be merely a place where people are walking past him engaged in their own affairs, attending to their business, going to their dismal little jobs and enacting their tiny ambitions. The Earth is now a game reserve, a free zone where anything is possible. Everywhere transactions are taking place. How much money is there in Buenos Aires on any single day? In people's pockets, in cash registers, in offices… in bank safes. It's a simple matter of making a minuscule portion of it land in his pocket. And he's going to figure out how: choose a target, calculate probabilities, scope out the scene, take measurements, calculate timing, find access and escape routes and carefully choose cohorts. He'll need brave but not reckless people. Must avoid psychopaths and murderers, find guys who like the good life, not those who enjoy making other people suffer. Killing and violence must be avoided. Intimidation is one thing; murder quite a different one. The dead are expensive, concrete; money, on the other hand, is abstract, worth only what you can buy with it and that's always in flux. Victims have friends, relatives who adore them, avengers who never forget. Life lost never returns; money can always be recovered. Money can also be given back or used to buy impunity. Death can only be avenged, and if it's the law that settles accounts, it's called justice. The only true revenge is the death of the killer. The chain can go on forever. Perhaps if Cain hadn't killed Abel there'd be no wars today. That's assuming, of course, that the story actually took place.

He's made three observations he considers important. One: many police stations are being renovated; they're surrounded by workers, materials, barriers and containers. Two: many banks are also being renovated; the scene is similar to that at the stations. Three, and this is a real boon: in a few days Independiente play the final match of the Intercontinental Cup against Liverpool in Tokyo. Miranda smiles. Rarely has there been such a favourable convergence. His mind soars as it catalogues each and every detail he must take into account in order to execute a plan that he's already sketched out in his head.

He walks back to his hideout. He arrives at that uncertain hour when daylight is still in the sky, but at street level it's already night. He carefully chooses the outfit he's going to wear and lays it out on the bed. Dark suit, white shirt, a Liberty of London flowery tie, a bit shabby but the flowers are still in bloom. Boxer shorts and cotton socks. He shaves, showers, dries himself off, douses himself in cologne, lies down in bed naked and turns on the television set. He likes to air himself out after bathing. Now he can do it, now that he has begun to enjoy his freedom. He turns on the TV and watches the new Chief of Police giving a press conference. In fact, he's talking precisely about the plans to renovate the local precinct stations in order to improve public service. The journalist points to a logo on a patrol car that reads: "To serve the community", which the chief says reflects the new philosophy that must infuse such an institution in a participatory and democratic society. The true change, Mole thinks, is in the way people talk. The language he uses sounds more educated, more refined. The police higher-ups no longer speak in street slang, they're starting to act more like politicians than policemen. He dozes off. Bernando Neustadt, the TV commentator, wakes him up with his sissy voice. He expresses his disappointment, he misses the iron fist of the armed forces. Miranda turns off the TV. He gets up and gets dressed. It's time to take his final exam, and he feels like he knows the material backward and forward.

From the shadows across the street he watches the students of Lía's Art Studios leave the building and walking away in groups of twos or threes, carrying their portfolios under their arms. Mole looks at his watch. It's a little after

61

ten at night. He waits two minutes, crosses the street and enters the building. From the foyer he can see Lía, who has not yet noticed his arrival. She has an asymmetrical haircut with a quiff of shocking-red hair falling over half her face. She's got a great body, and her lily-white skin is not marred by a mole, a freckle or even a spot, according to his memory of her body from very close range. Nobody would guess that this tiny woman is as powerful as a locomotive when she makes love. Miranda smiles with satisfaction; he feels his sex getting restless. Her unconditional loyalty to him seems a lot like love but also contains a good dose of gratitude, a rare virtue Mole values highly. He convinced her to give up prostitution, paid for her to take classes with a painter with an unpronounceable name, whom everyone called Bear, set her up in the studio and bought the equipment that allowed her to become what she is now, what she calls a plastic artist. Miranda thinks this is funny because, as far as he can tell, this girl hasn't a touch of plastic about her. Lía's charm sells more paintings than her brush and as a born survivor on her way to fame and fortune, she knows quite well how to deploy her virtues to their full advantage. Just as Lía starts to take off her apron, she sees him. She looks surprised, then freezes, then shoots him a sidelong glance out from under that cute red quiff. Then a smile, unreserved and also bright red, spreads out like a curtain to reveal a vaudeville of teeth, restless tongue and shining eyes.

Wow, this really is a surprise. Hi, Lía. It's been so long, how are you? What you see… I missed you. I was abroad. Yeah, I saw you on the news. Oh, you saw me. I saw you. You okay?

Perfect. The family? Very well, thank you. What's going on with your life? Do you have a minute? I've got all night.

Lía gives him a complicit smile and picks up the telephone.

Just a second, I have to arrange something. Hello, Clara, it's me... Yes... No, nothing... If Ricardo calls, don't answer your phone... I'm going to tell him you're having problems with your boyfriend and I'm going to see you... You witch, how did you guess?... You're evil... Anyway... we'll talk tomorrow.

She hangs up and dials again.

Ricky... Everything okay, honey?... Listen, don't come pick me up... No, nothing... It's just that Clara had a row with Roberto, she's really upset... You don't mind putting it off till tomorrow?... Sure?... Ooh, I wanted so badly to see you... You don't sound sad enough... I'll call Clara and tell her I can't... Sure?... Okay, that's fine... Let's talk tomorrow... Great big kiss... Okay. All squared away. Sure was easy for you to string him along. Not really, it's in his interest, he's married. Have you ever gone out with anyone who wasn't? I don't remember, I was very young. Where are you taking me? Shall we go eat? Let's. What do you feel like? I'll take you to a very "in" place. You'll like it.

With one quick movement, she grabs her leather jacket and her purse, then turns off the light. She motions to Miranda to go out of the door before her. She closes and locks it behind her, takes his arm and walks quickly with him to the corner. They turn up an alleyway and stop in front of a boarded-up house. Under an enormous rubber tree, Lía turns and plants a kiss on Miranda's mouth, which he reciprocates by putting his arms around her waist and pressing her against his body. Lía disengages, turns toward the main street and lifts her arm as gracefully as she possibly can. The taxi driver is young but the city has already poisoned his spirit. Lía is sitting next to Miranda, definitely pressing her thigh against his. Her aroma, the physical contact, the sound of Lía's voice awaken each and every cell in Mole's body, which is joyous and full of energy, anticipating the delights of this woman's body that he knows he's going to inhabit that very night when he's a bit lightheaded from the wine they'll have with their meal. The driver is listening to disco music at full volume. Lía gently strums her fingers against Miranda's hand to the beat of the music. They do not speak. The taxi driver derives some kind of neurotic pleasure from speed and his remarkable skill at swerving in and out between the traffic and the pedestrians. He drives with cunning, passing other cars along Avenida Corrientes, which, at that moment, is relatively deserted. He pulls into the lead and catches the green wave, never letting other drivers sneak into the empty spots at the corners between the cars that are waiting for the lights to change. All the while he is constantly checking to make sure no sleepwalker wanders into the road from one of the side streets, modulating his speed as he approaches each light. In mere minutes they have crossed the city from Colegiales to near the Plaza San Martín, where Lía takes him by the hand and leads him into Morizono, a Japanese restaurant where Mandrake the Magician's girlfriend prepares delicious rolls of raw fish with rice. Life has finally shaken itself awake. Prison has been left a thousand years behind.

9

Valli sees the sign from the freeway, takes the next exit, drives over the overpass and returns along the frontage road to Two Gold Coins grill. The last customers are still gorging themselves on pieces of mixed grill washed down with cheap wine. Horacio is stirring the coals and spreading them out to create the uniform heat he needs to finish cooking without burning a few large pieces of flank steak. Valli walks through the wood-framed opening hung with plastic that serves as a door. Fatso Horacio has left part of the grill without coals. That's where he piles up the grilled chorizos he'll heat up for that night's dinner. Valli walks up to the bar and sits down on one of the stools.

How're you doing, Boss? Where've you been hiding? I'm stopping by to pay you a visit. Wanna eat? Thanks, but I already did. I've got some grilled peppers with garlic that will make you lick your fingers up to your elbows. Another time. I've got a gig for you.

Horacio checks to make sure nobody is listening.

I heard Turcheli kicked the bucket. Heart attack. Right after his promotion. Tough luck. Who's going to take his place? Filander.

Can I come back? I don't know, we'll have to see. What you got for me? A hit, serious shit. Who? A former superintendent. Who? Lascano. Perro? The one and only. Didn't he die? Not even remotely. There was a gunfight with some soldiers, but he got away. No shit, somebody must have had his back. Who's protecting him? Protected him. Who? The one with the heart attack. Say no more, where do I find him? We're tailing him. You up for it? No problem, what's in it for me? Same as always, maybe a reinstatement, if everything works out. Everything will work out. Be careful, Perro's no pushover. Don't worry. You're the one who should worry. Everything's got to go just right. If you screw up or they nab you, you're going to be lonelier than Adam on Mother's Day. Have I ever screwed up? I don't know. You'll get me the gun? You get it yourself. Okay, okay, how much will you give me now? Five grand, will that do? That'll do. As soon as I hear, I'll let you know where he is. Done deal.

The next day Horacio parks his car in front of the Retiro bus terminal. Around his own neighbourhood, they call his Valiant II "The Panther" because of the of black spots showing through the yellow he painted on after he stole it. Horacio puts on the steering-wheel lock and walks into Villa 31, the shanty town. He turns down an alleyway and continues for about two hundred yards till he gets to the home of One-Eyed Giardina.

In 1965 anti-Peronist thugs organized a demonstration against Isabelita Perón, right in front of Hotel Alvear Palace in the middle of Barrio Norte, where she was staying. For a little spare change, Giardina signed up to be counted in this demonstration for the posh and privileged. But the plebs from the Infantry Guards beat the demonstrators with sticks and shot tear gas canisters at their heads. One of those canisters took out one of his eyes.

Horacio stops next to one of the hovels, in front of a paisley cloth curtain. He hears two men inside talking. He claps his hands. The voices stop. A moment later One-Eyed appears and invites him to come in. An ashen-faced man sits at a wooden table in front of a jug of red wine and a plate full of cubes of salami and cheese.

Sonia! Bring a glass for my friend.

A woman of undefined age appears from the next room, dragging her feet. She's missing her two front teeth and the rest of them are broken and yellowed. She looks Fatso up and down and slams the glass down on the table.

This is my buddy, José. What's up? Nothin' much. It's been a long time, Fatso. Yup, sure has.

One-Eyed looks at José and forces a smile. He serves Horacio some wine, then turns back to José and smiles.

Can we talk? My friend here was just leaving. Hey, no worries, I don't mean to rush you. Didn't I tell you he was just leaving? You were just leaving, weren't you? Yeah, it's getting late.

The goodbye ritual is short and sweet. After the man walks through the curtain, the other two check each other out during a long moment of silence. Finally, One-Eyed gets up, goes to the doorway, pulls back the curtain, looks up and down the alleyway and returns. He switches on the radio; a rasping cumbia is playing and he turns the volume way up.

Long time no see. You back in? Not yet. What're you up to? I opened a grill, you should come by one day. Where is it? Next to Acceso Oeste, right after the Morón exit. It's called Two Gold Coins; when you're heading into the city, it's on the frontage road on the other side. Where did you get that name? I opened it with the dough I made on a hit, a pretty-boy in a cabaret who had great big enormous eyes. When he saw he was done for, his eyes looked like two big gold coins.

One-Eyed's formidable laugh finishes up in a hacking cough that turns his one eye red; he pounds himself on the chest to quell it.

Man, you are nuts. What do you need? A twenty-two long. Good timing, I've got a jewel. What is it? It's not cheap. Show me. Wait here.

One-Eyed Giardina stands up, tells the woman to keep Horacio company and leaves. She sits down, lights a cigarette and stares at him while she fiddles with a box of matches. Horacio can't remember if he's seen her before or if she just reminds him of somebody else, but he knows that what he has in front of him is the ruins of a woman who once was beautiful. She still has some of a beautiful woman's gestures, something her appearance can't completely cancel out. Ten minutes later Giardina returns carrying a gun wrapped in a flannel cloth. The woman, clearly obeying rules long since established, immediately gets up and leaves. One-Eyed places the package on the table and lights a cigarette, motioning to Horacio to unwrap it. He slowly folds back the flannel. One-Eyed was telling the truth: there in front of him is a Ruger MK II .22LR semi-automatic stainless-steel pistol. Few guns are as well made as this one. It'll cost him a fortune, but it'll be well worth it. Light, trustworthy, he's never heard of one of these jamming. It has one feature that makes it the king of close-range shooting: the chamber is mounted on a system of springs that dampens the recoil from the detonation. The long barrel considerably reduces the report from this notably quiet pistol. To miss with this you'd have to be a real moron.

Seems you got yourself a good gig. You could say that. How much? Don't you want to try it? Don't need to, how much? Three grand, which includes one hundred hollow-pointed bullets. I've got two thousand. I guess you're out of luck. Don't fuck with me, how much will you give it to me for? Listen, you're not going to find anything like this anywhere else, but if I don't sell it to you today, I'll sell it tomorrow. How much? Not a peso less than two thousand eight. Okay, but on one condition. What? For the same price you drive my getaway car. Okay, who're you going to hit? A super. Do I know him? Bow-wow. Not Perro? Yup. In that case, not a peso less than three grand.

A few blocks from there, on Viamonte past Leandro Alem, Miranda is sitting and waiting for Bangs and Dandy at one of the tables in the back of El Navegante. He orders a bottle of Gancia wine and a plate of olives. He sees them enter: Dandy's fatter and Bangs is more nervous than ever. They join him at the table. Anybody seeing the three of them would think they were co-workers out on a dinner date. They order pork loin with chips *a la provenzal,* red wine and soda water. Dandy digs in, Bangs talks non-stop. Miranda observes: the crow's feet, the reading glasses, the slow reaction time, the unsteady hands, the hearing loss, the liver spots and that look of only slightly haughty resignation. Bangs speaks now with a lisp – his tongue is dual-tasking, making sure his dentures don't pop out. Dandy's movements are a lot less precise; he looks depressed, dispirited. The etchings time has left on his friends' faces are merely a reflection of the same on his own. He looks at the three of them in the mirror on the wall and asks himself: *I'm going to rob a bank with these buffoons?* The prospect does not inspire much confidence; on the other hand, he doesn't like the young ones. Those hoods are way too crazy, they snort a lot of blow, they want everything yesterday, they're greedy and strung out, they turn violent at the slightest excuse, and at the drop of a hat they'll stab you in the back or betray you without the least little qualm. He prefers old-school crooks, those who live by a code of honour, who aren't going to turn you in or sell you out for a couple of pesos. People with experience, who've been inside and know it's better to stay out. Like these two. Something can always go wrong, and time for robbery is always less than for murder. His plan is good, so good that he gets more and more excited as he spells it out to his accomplices, who also get excited just listening to him. His divine inspiration spreads a gold patina over all their regrets, which just a moment before had soured the scene with bitterness.

Here's the deal: the bank and the nearby police station are both undergoing renovations. The construction workers leave for lunch around one and return around two. Fifteen minutes past one, the three of us arrive dressed as workers. I've already scoped out a place where we can get the company's uniforms. You hang a sign in the door that says "Closed for Renovations" and stay put. Luckily most of the windows will be papered over for construction. You subdue the guard while I pack up the cash. At one thirty there are no squad cars on the streets. Especially not on that Monday when Independiente will be playing the final against the Brits. At the same time, another man will be blocking the police station parking lot with a truck, claiming he's got materials to deliver. While the duty cop goes to find out what's what, the guy driving the truck vanishes. We'll make the handbrake on the truck stick, which will give us a few extra minutes. The getaway car will be at the door of the bank. We'll be wearing suits and ties under our overalls. We'll leave them in the car. The driver will drop each of us off at a different place. We'll meet up three days later at a place I've already picked out.

The technical part of the discussion continues till midnight. They work out the details, weigh all the pros and cons. They decide that Mole will look after the loot and how they'll divvy it up. The most complicated part is choosing the team. The three of them trust and respect each other, but it won't be an easy matter to choose two others. One guy's inside, another's sick, the other's retired, they don't trust that one and that one's crazy. They deal out then discard one name after another and finally decide on Fastfingers to drive the getaway car. Valentín, a drama student, will drive the truck. Mole will be in charge of setting things up with them. Valentín will place the order at the lumberyard. A few minutes before the order leaves the warehouse, he'll show up and ask them to add a few things to it, then he'll get in the truck with the driver to show him the way. Their destination will be an abandoned house that has a long driveway to the back of the property. When they get there, he'll subdue him and leave him tied up in a shack in the back. Then he'll take the truck to the police station and act out the delivery scene.

Mole hands out a few thousand to make sure nobody gets into trouble before the day of the robbery. At the door to the restaurant, Bangs stops the first taxi that drives by.

Where're you kids going? I'm staying in the centre. I'm going to Haedo. I'll get you close. No, no problem, I want to walk a little.

Dandy starts down Leandro Alem, then turns down La Boca on his way to his dealer's house; he wants some good blow, not like that shit he sold him last time and that he'll have to make good on now. Miranda starts toward Retiro. He's going to scope out some weapons for the heist. He turns into Villa 31. When he's a few yards from his destination he sees someone coming out of the same shack he's headed for. Quickly, he slips down a side street and watches from the shadows as Horacio leaves. He can tell he's a cop in a split second. He watches him walk away whistling. Then he steps out of his hiding place, goes up to the curtain and claps his hands. When One-Eyed appears and greets him, the stench of cheap wine on his breath hits him in the face like a backhanded slap.

What's up, Mole? I'm right as rain, and you? Good, what brings you here? I'm looking for some equipment, but it looks to me like you're keeping some pretty questionable company lately. What are you talking about? The guy who just left. What's wrong with him? What do you mean, what's wrong? I can see the mark of the police cap on his forehead. He's out of the force. You don't say. I'm telling you. What did he want? We've got a gig. Oh, really. You'll be happy. Why? Let's just say it's the guy who nabbed you last time. You don't say. And when's that coming down? Don't know, soon. What do you need? Guns. Just tell me how many...

10

It's been two days since Ramona left him at a pension in Chacarita with a few australes, a bottle of analgesics and a lot of advice. She said she'd call or come by, but he hasn't seen hide nor hair of her and has no way of getting in touch. This morning the owner came to ask him how long he'd be staying because someone else was interested in the room. He also told him he'd have to pay in advance.

He counts the money he has left. He's got to do something, and he's got to do it now. He gulps down three aspirins, gets dressed and goes out without a clear idea where he's headed or what he's going to do once he gets there. He walks through the streets, trying to recognize this Buenos Aires that's shining in all its plastic splendour. The new economic policy, the Austral Plan, is basically just more of the same: a repeat performance of the *plata dulce*, or "sweet money" period during the dictatorship. Finally free from state terror, consumers are partying it up, officials are getting their knickers in a twist talking about democracy, and the majority say they never heard of the atrocities committed during the Dirty War. The dollar is worth less than the austral, and people are rushing all over the place trying to buy the very latest imported toys. Shop windows manage to look little better than a bad imitation of their cheapest American counterparts. The frenetic compulsion to buy is heightened by the unconscious certainty that this prosperity is fleeting. In the meantime, the faces of hunger and poverty that nobody seems to want to see are already showing up at the party. The captains of the financial sector accumulate capital as they gnaw constantly at the feet of the presidential throne where, buoyed up by his image as the champion of democracy, Alfonsín reposes in confidence.

He heads for the city centre. He's considering a visit to police headquarters; he's still got one friend in Criminal Records, but it may be too dangerous to get anywhere near the place. If the Apostles killed Jorge, he might be in their sights as well. Ramona's fear when she found out and the alacrity with which she washed her hands of him can only mean one thing: he's a marked man. She didn't say it in so many words, but it is implicit, and even if he was being paranoid, entering headquarters through the main door doesn't seem like the best way to find out.

He keeps walking till after one o'clock. He sits down on a bench in Plaza Lavalle. The effect of the aspirin begins to wear off, and the wound in his chest starts to hurt, less than yesterday though, *and more than tomorrow*, Lascano thinks in an unusual burst of optimism.

The shootout happened just a few blocks away; that was the day he saw Eva for the last time. He'd rented a safe deposit box at a nearby bank and put twenty thousand dollars in it. Eva had found the money by accident in a house she was hiding in when the military came to get her. Then, when all hell broke loose with Giribaldi and his death squad, they went to get the money so they could get out of town, but there they met Giribaldi's henchmen, right at the door to the bank, and that's when it all came down. The last thing he saw was Eva running away. *Did she manage to get the money? Maybe yes, maybe no. What if it all happened so fast she didn't have time, and she had to escape without it?* He knows he's desperately clutching at straws, out of necessity, because he can't come up with another idea. Someone he used to know, a guy named Fermín, worked at that bank. He decides to go there, only a few blocks away. When he gets there, he sees that there is, indeed, a bank. His memory of it, though, is quite different: the one he remembers had a kind of Soviet-style austerity and a different name. He goes in anyway. The safe deposit boxes used to be in the rear, almost within reach, the offices have made way for desks separated by carpeted partitions, and the tellers are all very young women dressed in uniforms of skirts and jackets, which look just like men's business suits with a touch of sexy "lite". Banks used to look like prisons; now they look more like a cross between a boutique and a brothel. The walls are covered with posters showing young men and women, smiling and prosperous, offering "package deals" with bombastic names, that include bank accounts, credit cards, *loans for the life you deserve.* Everything carefully designed to neatly package and tie up the customer. The deviousness here is so obvious that even the guy who designed the poster should be put in jail. On one side is the only office with glass walls. A small sign says "F. Martínez – Manager". Lascano lowers his eyes and meets those of Fermín, who looks at him as if he were seeing a ghost.

Lascano? How're you doing, Fermín? I see you got a promotion. Please, please, come in. I can't believe it. I saw you, dead, right here in front of the door. Well, I guess I wasn't that dead. I can't believe it. Start believing it.

It takes Fermín a good while to get over his shock. Lascano invents a story that will suit his temperament. Fermín is sincerely happy that Lascano has survived, this despite the fact that Lascano was the one who arrested him for robbery when he was a young man. Perro had rescued him, half dead from fear, right at the moment they were about to work him over, hard.

Look, Fermín, I'm here because I got this crazy idea. I don't know if you remember that I opened a safe deposit box. I remember very well. What happened to it, does it still exist? Nope. The bank changed ownership, I mean, just between us, the only thing that changed was the name and the decor. Then, when they started the construction that turned this into what you now see, they notified the owners of the inactive boxes and gave them a certain amount of time to come by the bank and close out their accounts. Those who didn't show up, their boxes were opened in front of a notary. I handled it personally. There were three or four, and one of them was yours. They were all empty. I see.

Perro looks down, the little wisp of hope vanishes without a trace, just as he suspected it would. Fermín notices.

Are you in trouble?

Sticking in bits and pieces of the true story, and seasoning it just right to prevent him from getting the idea that it would be dangerous to help him, Lascano spins a yarn about political rivalry within the department that, along with his gunshot wounds, left him on the street. He tells him he's hoping to recover the money that was in the safe deposit box, which no longer exists, and which, it appears, a treacherous female associate has stolen from him. When Lascano says "female associate" Fermín understands "lover", and he doesn't ask the amount or the source of the money. Nobody would ever think that a police superintendent would have a safe deposit box to stash his salary, and these days no banker is going to worry about where money comes from.

What are you planning to do? I've got a few job interviews. But it's not easy. These days, if you're over thirty-five you're all washed up.

They keep conversing until Fermín has to attend to an important client. They agree to meet another day after work, and Fermín tells him he'll see what he can do for him.

Even though Fermín came away thinking exactly what Lascano wanted him to, the visit brought about no tangible results. He needs to reflect, and walking is the best way he knows to do that. His world has shrunk even further. By now, he's got almost nothing left. With Jorge's death – whether brought about by the Apostles or a gift to them from Heaven – they won the battle. Chances are high that his own life's in danger. Suddenly he's overwhelmed by that same confused, diffuse and constant fear he had during the dictatorship, that sensation that at any moment he could be captured, tortured and killed. He doesn't know if his friend, Fuseli, and Eva, his too-brief lover, are in exile or if the military made them disappear. He wants to believe, he hopes, they managed to escape. Then, just as he turns down Corrientes, she appears: crossing the street diagonally toward him. He catches a brief glimpse of her profile as she walks by. Is it her? The air she stirs up as she walks past swirls around him. He feels like he's falling into the slipstream of foaming pheromones she leaves in her wake. Her catlike walk compels him to quicken his pace, like the cyclist who drafts behind a truck, taking advantage of the vacuum created by the movement of a body through space. Suddenly, she breaks into a trot to get to the bus waiting at the stop, and she boards. When she's on the stairs he calls out her name, she turns, it's her, it's not her. As this anonymous woman departs, Lascano sees the love of his life, love lost. He remembers Marisa's coffin being carried along the paths of the La Tablada cemetery, Fuseli's last words on the telephone, the foreshortened figure he saw from where he lay bleeding on the ground: Eva running away. That very real Eva who loved him one stormy night. Just when he thought he had nothing more to lose, she appeared, and from there unfolded the entire story that has brought him to this exact moment when he truly has nobody or nothing left. Lascano angrily pops two aspirins into his mouth and bites into them; the sound echoes inside his head like a pair of smashed and broken testicles.

11

He's been wandering aimlessly around the house ever since he woke up, out of sorts, unable to make sense of what he's doing, but finally it's the clock that gives him orders about how to proceed. He has to quickly get dressed. He hates rushing. Last night Vanina suggested they meet for breakfast. For her, it's always "we have to talk". She's always going on about their relationship, their connection. Marcelo has the impression that all those years of psychoanalysis poisoned her language and that "we have to talk" comes so frequently it can't be healthy, even though to her it seems the most natural thing in the world.

In the elevator, he presses his briefcase between his legs and finishes adjusting his tie. The outside world greets him with a massive traffic jam accompanied by a deafening symphony of insults and honking. *Buenos Aires drivers are a plague.* He looks at his watch and calculates that he'll arrive no less than ten or fifteen minutes late. He knows Vanina will wait for him, but only so she can tell him how angry she is, a privilege she allows herself because she herself is never late. To top it off he wants to get to the office early, he's got a ton of things to do, but as he didn't write anything down he's afraid he'll forget. Last night, on his way home from his mother's house, he had a breakthrough on the Biterman case. In a moment of inspiration he saw each and every step he needed to take as well as the order he should take them in – which is as important as the steps themselves. He told himself he was going to write it all down in his little grey notebook on his way to meet Vanina, but he has now decided to walk to avoid the traffic. To make matters worse, he knows that Vanina is going to come with demands, a pile of questions about their intimacy, and *what are we going to do about it*, and she'll make the whole thing so tangled and complicated that he'll be left totally in the dark. The light changes just as he gets to the corner of 9 de Julio, leaving him stranded. The avenue roars in front of him like a tsunami of metal bodies. He stares at the little man in the box, and waits anxiously for him to start blinking on and off. The only way to cross the widest avenue in the world on one light is to run. So Marcelo runs and keeps running till he gets to the corner of Corrientes and Uruguay, where Vanina will be waiting for him, a stone in each hand to throw at him. Not so long ago he played rugby, so he's in good enough shape to dash down these few blocks, using evasive manoeuvres to avoid all the other creatures in the judicial jungle who, at this hour of the day, are also rushing to be among the first to arrive at the courthouse. Half a block before El Foro he reduces his pace to a brisk walk, taking deep breaths to slow down his pulse. He tries to locate Vanina through the window, but he doesn't see her. He enters and looks for her at all the tables brimming with coffee cups, croissants, cigarettes, newspapers and legal briefs. She's not there. Were they supposed to meet here or in Ouro Preto? No, it was here, he's certain. A young female lawyer, wearing a very tight pin-striped blue suit, gets up to leave, prompting a wave of greedy stares. She walks by him, her breasts pushing against the buttons of her white blouse, stretching the buttonholes and producing a gap through which he glimpses the delicate lace of her brassiere. She leaves in her wake a cloud of sickly sweet perfume, easily compensated for by the sight of her hips' enchanting ability to slip between the tables. Marcelo sits down in the chair she has just vacated. He can feel the warmth of this fantastic woman's body that still permeates the vinyl.

He orders a *cortado*, an espresso with a little hot milk, and takes his grey notebook out of his pocket. He's grateful that Vanina is late. It gives him the opportunity to jot down some notes and offers him impunity from her reproaches for his habitual lateness, at least this time.

Twenty minutes later he arrives in his office. He picks up the telephone and calls Vanina's house. The line is busy. He takes off his jacket, hangs it up, opens his briefcase, takes out the envelope of the Biterman case, his grey notebook and Kelsen's book, and places them on his desk, sits down, calls Vanina again. It's still busy. He opens his notebook, picks up the telephone, presses the buttons with the eraser of his yellow-and-black Pelikan pencil.

Assistant Superintendent Sansone?... Pereyra here... Very well, thank you, and you?... Do you have something for me?... When was that?... Are you sure?... What's the girl's name?... Who told you?... Where is she?... If we call her in as a witness, will she come?... I understand... You don't say... Where can I find that doctor?... He told you he gave... What do you mean he himself asked for it?... In Martínez?... But the girl was already pregnant when they captured her... Could anyone be such a son of a bitch?... No, of course, I know... Do we have an address?... Wait a minute... Go ahead... Yes... Yes... Good. One more thing... Do you know Superintendent Lascano?... Yes... Really?... But he got away... Where can I find him?... I understand... If you see him tell him to call me, I want to talk to him about the Biterman case... Thanks... I'll let you know if I hear anything else...

Marcelo stares at the name and address he just wrote down in his grey notebook. It is the same address, where he took the envelope to Giribaldi? He doesn't think he can tie him to the whole string of murders the military committed to cover their tracks, but he's planning to use the information to pressure him and get some information about the whereabouts of several children "appropriated" during the dictatorship. There are three pieces of evidence that would tie everything up and finish the package with a flourish. One: find the weapon Biterman's murderer had put in hock at the Banco Municipal. All the information he needs for that is in the envelope. Two: interview the witness the military kidnapped in Martínez. Three: find Lascano.

He leans back in his chair, places the pencil between his teeth. He is happy because his investigations are finally bearing fruit, but that sensation is quickly replaced by another: the revulsion he feels at being happy about solving cases that are so utterly abhorrent. Then he remembers Vanina, picks up the telephone, and calls her parents.

12

This morning Miranda has come to this working-class neighbourhood in Villa Del Parque dressed as a construction worker. He's sitting down in the street and leaning against a wall, his legs crossed and his yellow hard hat pulled down to his eyes, spying on the house where his wife and son live. Fernando, his son, is the first to leave. He's on his way to school. Mole is both distressed and pleased to see how much the boy has grown; such a short time ago he was just a child. For some reason he can't quite figure out, he's putting off his encounter with him. Fernando takes out a Walkman and turns it on. He puts the earphones in his ears and places the player in a small pouch attached to his belt. Miranda remembers that at his age he carried a gun in the same place. He waits. He hasn't yet seen any signs of men hanging around. Not during the day or at night, when Fernando goes out and she stays home alone. In the room on the first floor, at about ten at night, the blue light of the TV goes on, and less than an hour later it goes off, and nothing else happens all night. Duchess goes out very little, and then only to buy groceries. Sometimes, in the afternoons, she gets a visit from Pelusa, the neighbour who lives on Pasaje El Lazo, and they sit in the kitchen drinking maté.

Susana leaves the house and walks toward Jonte. Miranda stands up and follows her. She's walking in front of him in her flowered housedress. He knows all too well what's beneath that innocent-looking article of clothing. The whole time inside he was longing for that body, and now he has it, right here, almost within reach. His plan is to show up tomorrow, then take things from there. There's no other man in the picture, he's made sure of that. She stops at the grocery store, then the greengrocer's. When she enters the butcher's shop, Miranda keeps walking till he gets to the bus stop. The sun's reflection off the shop window of La Vaca Aurora doesn't let him see what's going on inside, but he can watch the door from where he is now.

When she enters, Pepe looks up and smiles at her. She lowers her eyes and waits for him to finish attending to her neighbour. After his wife died he started looking at her in a different way. He always gives her the feeling he's about to say something but that he never quite musters the courage. They've known each other for years, he knows who her husband is, and maybe that frightens him off. He used to be bolder before his wife died; he flirted with all his women customers, flattered them and shot them suggestive glances. Now he seems more reserved; he must feel more vulnerable. Through the curved glass of the display case, Susana watches him work. He plunges an old knife that is by now almost all handle into the sirloin steak on the wood slab. With quick confident movements he hones the new knife with the sharpening steel. He places his hand flat down on the meat and starts slicing off cutlets with highly skilled precision, each movement identical, each slice the same thickness, all falling gracefully one at a time in a neat stack that mimics the original shape of the steak. *You said a kilo?* He asks her only as an excuse to talk to her, only so she'll look up at him, only so their eyes will meet. She does so briefly, and nods. Will he ever summon the courage to say something to her, to ask her out? He doesn't believe she'll say yes, but he keeps asking her with his eyes. He keeps asking her when the scale reads a kilo and a quarter, and he charges her for only a kilo. And she feels flattered, he makes her feel beautiful, desired; she likes it. She walks out with her skirt swaying just a little more than usual, carrying with her the butcher's gaze, glued upon her.

That night, impeccably groomed and dressed to the nines, Miranda arrives at the house and waits patiently until the door opens and Fernando leaves. Duchess says goodbye to him from the doorway, where she continues to stand as she watches him disappear around the corner. That's when Mole crosses the street and rings the doorbell.

I thought you'd never come. Well, here I am. You sure took your time. I had things to arrange. You've been spying on me? A little. Are you going to invite me in or are you going to bring the chairs out here for us to sit on in the street? Come in. Fernandito is old. Yeah, so are we. Time waits for no man. What are your plans? I have some business to take care of…

They're both thinking that some things, no matter how you look at them or twist and turn them around, simply can't be fixed.

… Look, I don't want to know anything, but this can't go on. But I haven't said anything yet. When you say you have some business, I know I'll soon see your picture in the papers. I'm tired of this, Duke, of living with a lump in my throat and a prayer on my lips. This time it'll be different. Don't give me that crap, it's always different and it's always the same. No, Duchess, I swear, this time'll be different. I'm going to start a business, we're going to live well, without all the hullabaloo, on this side of the law. A business… what kind of business? You've never been in business. I'm going in with a guy… don't look at me like that, he's got nothing to do with that world, he's a Jew who imports kitchen appliances. We're going to open a first-class shop downtown. You've got to believe me. Are you staying? I don't know, are you inviting me? You hungry? A little. Come to the table.

While Duchess is in the kitchen preparing him a bite to eat, Miranda notices she's wearing her high heels. She was waiting for him. She knew. Duchess always knows. This is the woman he wants, hers the body he desires, she his partner, his perfect fit, with whom two becomes one. His memory brings back everything now hidden under that tight dress, which is a bit bold, provocative and modest all at once. Miranda knows that when that dress comes off, the other Duchess appears. Wise, receptive, generous, a duchess who's not disgusted by anything and can do it for what seems like an eternity, capable of carrying him to the highest peaks of arousal only to lower him gently, again and again, as many times as she wants, leading him from the valleys to the mountains with sure hands through the steep curves, boldly bordering the cliffs until finally she releases him and lets him come inside her – open, satisfied, languid, happy, adored. He can imagine nothing better than coming in her arms. Miranda has been with many women in his life, but not one gives of herself so fully in bed. She offers up her entire being because she is one of those rare women who derives her own pleasure from the other's pleasure, her happiness from that of her companion.

What are you looking at? I'm looking at you. Don't get your hopes up, it's not going to be easy. I'm hooked on you. We'll have to correct that. You're right, when do we start? Get your hand out of there. Remember when you used to say, "You've got half an hour to get your hand out?" Now you've got half a second. A minute? Get it out. Just a little, sweetheart, I've missed you so much. No, really, we have to talk. I don't want to live this way any more. Me, neither, I swear. I found out about Noelia's illness. How? The last time Screw came to bring me money he was almost collapsing, and all I had to do was say one word and it all came gushing out like a broken water main, the whole story in one big burst. Poor guy is a mess. He also told me you were about to get out and that I probably wouldn't see him for a while. He seemed afraid. Of course, how could he not be afraid? I mean, not about his daughter, but about you. Me? Why would he be afraid of me? I think he spent all your money. I saw Screw, I know everything, and everything's been worked out. Yeah, but you don't have any money. What are you going to use to start your precious business? Someone's going to loan it to me. Listen, Duke, I don't want to know anything about it. I love you, you know that, but I can't take it any more. I can't stand knowing your life is in danger or that you're going to spend the next few years in jail. We're not twenty any more. Eduardo, promise me, swear to me that you aren't going to arrive

*home with the police following you. I live with my heart in my
mouth. Every time the doorbell rings I think they're coming to
tell me you've been killed. You know I've forgiven you forevery-
thing, but I would never forgive you if they killed you in front
of Fernando. I know I can't ask you to go buy the newspaper
and look for a job. Duchess, you've got to trust me. I love you
and Fernando more than anything else in the world. Give me
a chance to sort things out, then I'll stop forever, all I want is
a peaceful life. Oh, Duke, I'm so worn down I don't even have
it in me to think things through...*

Silence settles over the kitchen, one of those marital
silences that hovers in the air like the poisonous vapours
from a swamp. It's an uncomfortable, painful silence
that conjures up all past frustrations, allowing all the
disappointments and sorrows to appear one by one,
while amnesia makes all the once-shared joy vanish.
Duchess is looking at him as if from behind a glass wall
or from a thousand miles away, and all she feels is fear.
Fear of her own feelings, fear of having regrets, fear of
what she's going to say and, more than anything, fear
of continuing to feel fear. She feels as if she still doesn't
have the words she wants to say to this man she loves so
much. She feels all dried up, dry and tired. Her voice
is pleading.

*Right now I want you to go. Don't do this to me, Duchess. What
do you think, that I don't want it too? For four years I haven't
had any either. Sort things out, as you say, then come back and
we'll see. Okay, you're right. Just remember one thing: this is the
last time, Duke, the very last time.*

Her words evoke the possibility that he'll be gunned down one day by the police, an echo of his own conviction about his fate, the one he usually manages to shunt away. He also understands what Duchess didn't say, but the message, a stern warning, was right there, behind her words. If what she said were to happen, she would let the city bury him, she'd never mention him to their son and, when his flesh rotted away, his bones would be thrown into a common grave, without a flower or a tear, without anything. That, for Mole, would be worse than death itself. The life he has led has kept him away from his son for long stretches at a time, and that's what has always troubled him most about his profession as a bank robber. If, in addition to this, he were forever erased from Fernandito's memory, even he would never forgive himself.

13

Maisabé is rushing around; she wants to leave before Leonardo arrives. The ringing of the telephone makes her nervous, she picks it up, says hello several times, but nobody's on the other end. There are more and more of these dead calls every day. Her husband says it's the communists, who have come back. She walks across the living room and looks out the window to see how people are dressed, if it's hot or cold outside. She looks in at the door to Aníbal's bedroom: he's sitting at his desk looking at a picture book. He's so little and always so serious, so absorbed in whatever he's doing, so quiet, so indifferent. The child seems not to even notice her presence, but when she walks away down the hallway, he noiselessly gets up and watches her as she enters her bedroom. He takes four steps and stops in the precise spot where the mirror of the coat rack reflects off the one on the closet door, in which Maisabé is looking at herself. She takes out a red paper bag and empties it on the bed. Out falls a pink lace bra and panties. She stops and stares at them, a strange smile on her face. She drops the shower towel she has wrapped around her, puts on the underwear and looks at herself in the mirror, making a pout that wants very much to be sensual. The boy returns to his room.

Maisabé finishes getting dressed. From the back of a drawer she pulls out a small blue perfume bottle and a blood-red lipstick and puts them both in her purse. She puts on a jacket and calls to Aníbal. They leave the building. Sitting at a table at the bar on the corner, Leonardo Giribaldi watches them cross the street and turn the corner toward the stop where they'll catch the bus to the parish church. He doesn't want to see them or for them to see him. He pays for his coffee, walks out, crosses the street and enters the building.

Ten minutes later Maisabé and Aníbal enter the patio of the parish church. Father Roberto, who prefers to be called just plain Roberto, is conversing with some other mothers. As usual when she sees him, Maisabé feels a shiver up and down her spine and a hot blush on her cheeks. He notices it and gives her a scintillating look. Aníbal lets go of her hand and walks toward the catechism classroom, as if he were on his way to the gallows. Graciela is hogging Roberto's attention, jabbering on and on like a blonde parrot. Maisabé walks toward them but Leonor stops her on the way. She wants to invite Aníbal to her son's birthday party. She hands her an invitation decorated with little teddy bears and colourful balloons. Roberto is wearing jeans and a white shirt. The jeans are bell-bottoms, already out of fashion, but they look fantastic on him. Maisabé imagines him naked and herself in her new underwear, in front of him, under him, on top of him. As if he'd heard her summons, he starts to walk toward her. Her knees are shaking. Roberto touches her arm gently, Maisabé's skin absorbs the warmth from his hand as desert sands do from the sun. She blinks slowly – in fact, she

94

wants to close her eyes so as to better hear the music of his words. When she opens them, she sees only his mouth. A thin line of saliva, which she longs to lick, gleams between his lips. Roberto is looking deeply into her eyes. Graciela approaches. She brazenly takes his hand and tells him that there's something she must show him. *What an idiot I was!* When Roberto asked who would help him organize the bazaar, Maisabé was daydreaming, just like now, and that fake blonde beat her to it. Now that bitch has the perfect excuse to see him five times a week. In addition, with all that rushing around, she forgot to put on her perfume and lipstick. Now it's too late, now there's no point.

She sits down alone on one of the benches on the patio and keeps her eyes glued on the closed door of the sacristy. She's daydreaming. A short while later the door opens and the two of them emerge. Her hair is mussed, just a little, almost nothing. The buckle on Roberto's belt has slid a little to the right. She wonders if they were making out in there, and immediately the scene plays itself out in her imagination. The two of them on the oak desk, surrounded by sorrowful images of saints, passionately groping each other, kissing with serpentine tongues, hands burrowing under clothing, moaning and, suddenly, surprise surprise, she sees herself in the same scene, approaching them, squeezing in between those two bodies that press against hers... She opens her eyes and realizes that her new panties are moist. From the other side of the patio, Roberto is looking at her. She feels her face flushing, she looks down and pretends to be looking for something in her bag, but the only thing she finds in there is her lipstick.

The children come out of the classroom and run around the patio, chirping like little birds. Aníbal is the only one who doesn't join in. He walks up to her and stares, as if he knew. The other mothers stand around and listen attentively to the priest, who talks to them with a big smile and calm, deliberate gestures. Maisabé gives a sad wave and moves toward the door. Roberto excuses himself and intercepts her. He looks at Aníbal, tenderly caressing his head. Maisabé stares at those voluptuous fingers lingering on the child's hair. With one quick move, Aníbal repels his touch.

Aníbal, wait for your mama by the door, I'd like to talk to her for a moment.

The child looks at them with total indifference and walks away.

Maisabé, we have to talk.

Roberto's eyes are shining as if he'd been reading her thoughts this whole time. Or could she be imagining it?

Talk? Tuesday is the best day. Tuesday? I'll meet you here at twelve.

Roberto touches her hand and smiles. She quickly nods and walks to the door. She feels like she's levitating, just as she did the first time she met him.

Aníbal looks out the window of the bus. He watches the people walking down the street. He counts, he looks around, he plays.

Green. One, two, three, four, five, six, seven... a woman with a green coat. Yellow. One, two, three, four, five, six, seven, eight, nine, ten, eleven... a man with a yellow raincoat...

Sitting next to him, Maisabé stares dreamily at the floor, happy and guilt-ridden for what she is feeling. The bus starts filling up. She watches the dance of the passengers' feet as they squeeze more and more tightly into the aisle, their bodies pressing and rubbing against each other to the rhythm of the swaying, the braking, the potholes. She feels exhausted. She puts her hand in the pocket where she carries her rosary and turns it around with her fingers as she does when she prays, but she isn't praying, she just uses it to quiet the trembling in her hand or, at least, to simulate prayer. What she wants to do is think about Roberto.

María, we're home.

She snaps to. Aníbal has never called her Mama, or Maisabé, as everyone else calls her, not even María Isabel, as she was baptized. He calls her plain María. He's got something with names; he doesn't call Giri "Papa" or "Leo", either. He calls him Giri, like his fellow officers do, or Sir, like the soldiers under his command, when he had some. If adults ask him his name, he doesn't answer, he pretends he's deaf or he looks at her, so she'll answer for him. She has, however, been told that when children at school or church ask him his name, he says Juan. Once she asked him why, and he refused to answer. He always does what he's asked, he never talks back, or complains, he obeys as if his life depended on it. At two, when he

97

was asked for a kiss, he'd say, "All done"; at four he began to dress himself; at six he was already deciding what he would wear every day. He wants to do everything by himself and seems vexed when someone offers to help. He does well in school, not the best student but not the worst, staying right in the middle of the curve where he is protected on both ends from the mediocrity of his teachers. He gets along well with his classmates, and he's fairly popular, which strikes the teachers as odd, because he never smiles or laughs with adults, whom he keeps under strict surveillance. Many of them feel intimidated by his eyes that seem to burrow into them and rummage through all their secrets.

In the meantime, Giribaldi opens the drawer, unfolds an orange flannel cloth, takes out a wooden box, places it on the desk and opens it. Inside lies a black Glock 17 with its Storm Lake barrel and its magazine with seventeen rounds. Next to it he places the cleaning kit with its bronze brushes, cleaning rag and the little bottle of lubricant, which is almost empty. He places the pistol on the flannel cloth. He presses the button that releases the magazine, removes all the bullets and lines them up one by one as if they were toy soldiers. He draws back the slide and makes sure no bullet is left in the chamber. He removes the barrel and the slide exposing the recoil spring assembly. With a watchmaker's screwdriver he pushes down the plastic spacer. He puts on his reading glasses. The next step requires enormous care because the spring is being held at maximum tension. When he disengages the safety catch it might shoot toward his face. It could easily take out an eye. This is not a toy, it is a killing machine and this condition is present in every one of its mechanisms. Giri manipulates the spring clip with great precision. He removes the hammer, then the trigger housing with the ejector, then presses down and holds the small silver safety button. He turns the extractor until he can remove it from the slide, then disengages the safety catch. He lines up all the pieces and looks at this orderly array. One drop of sweat falls off his forehead and draws a big yellow sun on the orange cloth. At this moment it is an innocent mechanism, incapable of causing harm. If someone attacked him right now, he would be unable to defend himself, for the individual parts pose no danger at all. Freed from its internal tensions, it is nothing more than a collection of greased metal parts designed to fit together perfectly. With great care he dips the tiny brushes in the cleaning solvent and goes over each piece thoroughly. He lubricates the moving parts then removes all the excess oil with the rag. Now comes the part he likes best. He pauses for a moment to memorize the exact location of each and every cleaned and oiled piece on the flannel cloth, starts the stopwatch on his wrist, closes his eyes and reassembles the pistol at top speed. He opens his eyes, looks at his watch – eighteen seconds – and smiles. He picks up the magazine and places it on the table. He polishes the bullets one by one before loading them. When he's done, he inserts the magazine into the receiver in one energetic movement. Even though a pistol never loses its power to intimidate, it's only when it is assembled and loaded that it takes on its full destructive capability. He grips it, then points it at the heads of the people in the pictures one by one: General Saint Jean handing him his diploma; his father; himself as a cadet; Maisabé dressed for her first communion; Aníbal at the beach with his sour face. The weapon feels light and strong, powerful. He cocks it, it's ready to shoot; this is the decisive moment, the tiniest movement of his middle finger resting on the sensitive trigger is all that separates whoever dares defy or disobey him from eternity. The only real power is that of life or death over other people.

He hears the elevator arrive, the doors open, the key being inserted into the lock. Aníbal walks by his door and says hello without looking at him. Three seconds later, Maisabé is standing in the doorway. The Glock is resting on Giri's lap, where his wife cannot see it.

How are things? Good. How did it go? To tell you the truth, this business of taking Aníbal to catechism school precisely at rush hour is enough to earn me my place in heaven. I thought you'd already earned it. Are you hungry? A little. There's steak. Good. Salad or mashed potatoes? Whatever you like. Okay.

As she enters the kitchen, she has an attack of silent rage against her husband. The remains of a ham sandwich on the kitchen counter has turned into a restless mass of ravenous ants. Maisabé hates these industrious and tiny insects that, in all the years they've lived in this apartment, they've never managed to exterminate. She picks up a small pot, turns on the hot water tap and places the pot under it. With a familiar groan, the flames of the instant hot-water heater spread a blue hue over her movements, and as the pipes heat up the water they emit a painful cry. While the pot fills with water she observes the ants carrying their crumbs, rushing to and from the food, crossing paths, stopping briefly, as if to chat. They are ruled by an orderly frenzy. She places the pot next to the edge of the counter and, using a kitchen towel, pushes the sandwich and the ants into the pot. The insects stop moving the second they touch the hot water. She, on the other hand, can touch it without getting burnt very much at all. She throws the water and the dead ants down the sink, picks up the remains of the wet bread and ham and throws it in the trash can. The hot water streaming out of the tap washes the cadavers down the drain, and the yellow rag finishes up those who are dispersed and disoriented, dazed. One last ant crawls around the counter in circles. Maisabé looks at it and, once it finally decides on a direction, smashes it with her thumb, the exoskeleton making a cracking sound as it breaks. She looks at the remains, the internal organs squished on her fingertip, and she is tempted to put it in her mouth. Instead, she rinses it off under the water. She takes out the cutting board and places a slab of meat on it. She picks up the wood meat pounder and brings it down on the meat, watching as the small veins break apart and the meat fibres bleed.

Her mind travels to a future after Giribaldi is dead, Aníbal has left and Roberto... *who knows?* She imagines herself alone in the world, alone in life, making the first, only, and last free choice: to swallow an entire bottle of sleeping pills. In her mind's eye she sees herself as an old woman, lying down on her bed to die. She sees herself dead. The ants, in patient procession, come to devour her. Her body will be communion for those indefatigable creatures whose only god is hunger. By the time someone finds her, there will be nothing left

101

but bare bones; her flesh will have become part of that despicable army of obedient and minuscule beings who will remain in the house to torment its next residents as they have tormented her. In the end, the ants will be the victors, no matter how many she kills.

14

Alone. Lost. Confused. Wandering the streets. Surrounded by rushing strangers. Pursued. Hunted. Dressed as a construction worker and carrying a bag loaded with disorderly bundles of dollar bills. Trying to catch his breath, to calm down. Trying, without success, to quiet the wild beating of his heart, which is making him dizzy. Gasping for breath. The sirens of the police cars bounce off the buildings full of respectable white-collar workers. The adrenaline courses through his blood, prevents him from thinking, readies him for only fight or flight. Rage clouding his vision. His awareness that this state of mind is his perdition. Just when he feels his last edge of sanity cracking under his step, thunder echoes and it begins to pour. Strong, furious, as if it will never cease. A dense, ferocious rain, one that seems determined to wipe the human race off the face of the Earth. A rain that slows the rush and increases anxiety, that destroys the makeshift hovels of the poor and spoils the parties of the rich. A rain that forces suits paid out in six instalments to take refuge under the eaves and balconies, and their contents to look up to the sky, begging for a reprieve that will allow them to get to work on time. That's when Miranda the Mole begins to walk under the downpour. Refreshed, renewed, composed. He thinks about Duchess. As if she had sent him this storm to abate the squall within. He walks for blocks like that, calmly, until he enters the mouth of the underground. He lets the first train go by. The platform is momentarily deserted. He stands behind the newspaper stand, takes off his soaking-wet overalls and stuffs them under the stand. His suit has yellow stains on it.

When he re-emerges at Primera Junta station, the rain has turned into cold, sharp needles. He enters a second-rate clothing shop. He leaves behind him, to the astonishment of the sales people, a trail of water that could almost have been blood.

In the changing room he takes off his stained clothes, puts on some new ones, and dries the bag off with the old. In this minuscule space of privacy he slips his thirty-eight under his belt, takes out ten bills of a hundred dollars each, puts four in one pocket and six in the other. He bundles up his used clothes and stuffs them under a broken-down stool. He ignores the salesman who helped him and walks resolutely up to the cash register, where a smarmy man is doing some bookkeeping. He's the one in charge. You can tell because he looks like a rat. Miranda places six bills on the counter, in piles of two, two and two.

These two are for the clothes. Give me two hundred australes for these two. These two are so you'll keep your mouth shut.

He subtly adjusts his jacket to show his weapon.

If you ever saw me, I'll come back and kill you. Understand?

The rat immediately evaluates the deal on the counter: just one of those Franklins pays for the clothes and one more covers the amount of Argentinean money the man wants. He nods, picks up the six bills with his effeminate fingers, and stuffs them into his pocket; then he opens the register and places three bills of fifty australes and five of ten on the counter. He turns back to his bookkeeping as if Mole didn't exist. He never saw him.

Goodbye, sir, thank you very much.

Miranda walks out slowly. Along the way, he picks a raincoat off the rack, pulls off the price tag and throws it on the ground. Once outside, he trots to the corner, and with one small shove steals the only free taxi away from an elderly gentleman.

Where to, sir? Just drive. I'll tell you in a minute.

On the radio they're talking about Percudani's goal that beat the Brits in Tokyo. Miranda pays no attention to the driver's enthusiastic remarks.

Take me on a little tour. Anywhere you want, other than the centre.

The driver looks at him through the rear-view mirror. *Why did I have to get this deadbeat?* He decides to ignore his passenger and starts driving slowly down Rivadavia, in the right lane, adding his horn to the general uproar.

Unconcerned, Mole watches the wet city go by while he tries to work things out: first, where to hide the bag with the money; and then, where to hide himself. The robbery was a disaster, as usual, the victim of happenstance. A plainclothes cop, hoping to get his picture in the papers, was waiting in line at window 6. He'll be there in the afternoon edition, photographed in a pool of his own blood. The idiot drew his nine millimetre, but so clumsily that it fell on the ground, right at Dandy's feet. He doesn't understand why fat people have a reputation for being so calm. Dandy lost his head and shot him straight in his chest with his sawn-off twelve gauge, and for no reason at all because the copper was already unarmed. He had the advantage, but he killed him anyway. Bad nerves. The cop jumped back when the shells tore into his chest, then crumpled onto the ground. People started shouting as if they were all getting killed. Then Dandy shot into the air to make them shut up. Damn fool – a piece of plaster the size of a large pizza fell on him. Fastfingers, waiting in the getaway car at the door, heard the shots, put it in gear and hightailed it out of there. Mole had already packed up the loot, so he closed up the bag and pushed the dazed Dandy outside. When they got to the door, he told him to run in one direction and he took the other. In these cases, the best thing to do is separate. As he ran away, Mole managed to see Dandy slip, dropping his shotgun as he fell, at the precise instant a patrol car drove onto the sidewalk – two policemen grabbed him, and one knocked him out with a punch to his jaw. Mole's last glimpse was of Bangs running across the street.

A fuck-up, a major fuck-up. But that's life. Even when you've got the whole thing planned out to the very last detail, unexpected things happen, and then there's a chain reaction that ends up making a mess of everything. Or, as his grandfather used to say, *when things are in a mess, the tip of the turnip points up.* At least he came away with some cash, even if the bag with the money weighs three tons at the moment. He's got to think fast, hide out somewhere until things calm down. Which isn't going to happen anytime soon. Back in the bank there's a dead cop, and the police don't like that at all, they always think it could have been one of them. He doesn't have much faith in Dandy if they put pressure on him, which he assumes they'll do. He considers running off to Rosario, but he immediately discards that idea. Loro Benítez got nabbed a week before, and the Reverend is still breathing, barely and only as long as they don't unplug him. *Hell of a life I lead. Lía? No, Dandy knows her.*

As he rides down towards the Avenida San Martín bridge, he's already shuffled and discarded almost every possible place to hide. He decides to return to the one he has in the hopes that he hasn't been followed for the last couple of days. He doesn't think so, but you can never be sure.

15

Walking through the heart of the banking district, known as La City, Lascano feels alienated, as if Buenos Aires didn't belong to him, as if an army of headless suits had taken over. The invaders are around thirty years old; they wear grey suits and loud ties. They keep their eyes peeled straight ahead of them, speak only to each other, have cords hanging out of their ears, and wouldn't move aside even if their dying grandmother were trying to get through. Who are all these people, where did they come from all at once, and what happened to them? They go in and out of huge glass buildings. Some wear colourful backpacks, many haven't shaved for a couple of days, most take refuge behind large sunglasses, all of them are in a hurry. They are insolent, shout when they speak and call each other *boludos*, or morons. As he walks down 25 de Mayo toward the business centre of the city, the crowd of *boludos* becomes denser and denser, more compact. He's looking for the address he wrote down on a piece of paper; it must be one of these glass monoliths. In the lobby are two dark-skinned toughs dressed up in sheriff costumes, the little star badge and all. They look at all the men as if they want to punch them and at all the women as if they were about to rape them, but nobody looks at them, except others with the same colour skin. One of the cowboys is guarding a row of turnstiles in front of the elevators. Lascano watches as they all open the turnstile with the card they wear hanging off their waists. Modern shackles for these corporate slaves, he muses. The Turnstile Sheriff points him to a round counter where there's someone who looks like the marshal in a Hollywood Western – though this one's a Mapuche Indian. After a brief exchange and several longish pauses, he gives him a pass card and tells him to return it when he leaves, as well as a piece of paper on which he must get the signature of the person he is going to see. Now he's absolutely certain: this is a prison. He gives the guard at the turnstile a smile, but the other makes no sign of having received it; *he must be studying how to be a* boludo. The card lets him through and he enters the elevator, where five uncomfortable-looking *boludos* have already taken up residence. One of them looks him up and down, as if wondering what this guy is doing here. Finally, the elevator vomits him out into a hot, carpeted corridor lit by small lightbulbs. On the wall is a huge reproduction of the bank's logo. He walks up to the door and rings the bell, another light turns on and above his head a tiny closed-circuit TV camera focuses in on him.

Good morning. Lascano here to see Mr Fermín Martínez. Please come in.

As he opens the door he notices that it is much heavier than it seems. There to greet him is a girl dressed in a blue suit that matches the carpeting and the wallpaper. She's gorgeous and, in spite of how very young she is, she's known it for quite some time. She was probably born knowing it. She invites him to follow her, much too conscious of the effect of the swinging of her hips when she walks. She leaves in her wake an invisible cloud of imported perfume one could easily plunge into and sail away to one's final destiny. Turning around like a model on a catwalk, she points to some blood-red real-Russian-leather chairs and asks him if he would like something to drink. Perro says no and stares at her as she walks over to her desk, where she sits down, crosses her legs and checks to make sure she is being admired. She regales him with the mere hint of a smile that looks a bit like polystyrene. There's a small lamp above the armchair where Lascano sits down, which seems to have been placed there expressly to fry his brain, his feet grow warm through the carpet, ambient music comes faintly to him from somewhere, and every once in a while, a little peep...

Mr Martínez will see you now.

He opens his eyes to the vision of the torso and upper legs of the girl who is standing over him and smiling. He feels ashamed. If he knew he'd been waiting for half an hour, he'd be cross.

Forgive me, I fell asleep. I wish I could do the same. Follow me, please.

The office overlooks the renovations going on at the docks. The Rio de la Plata stretches out beyond: brownish grey, slow, treacherous. Fermín is standing next to a man

111

with bright white hair, who's sitting at the desk looking at something Fermín is showing him on a piece of paper.

Come in, Lascano, come in. I'd like to introduce you to Mr Makinlay.

The white-haired man stands up and reaches his hand out as Perro approaches the cherry-wood desk. His clothes alone are worth not a penny less than five thousand dollars, without counting the gold cufflinks, the watch and all the other trinkets. He speaks in a very refined voice, the voice of a man accustomed to dealing with kings; he himself looks like royalty. And he smiles as if he were on vacation in the Bahamas.

Mr Lascano, Fermín has spoken very highly of you. I understand you are a police superintendent. I was. Not any longer. Even better. He also tells me you are the best detective of the Federal Police. Tell me what you need and I'll tell you if I can do it. Agreed. Let's get straight to the point, then. Please do. There was a robbery at one of our branches. Uh-huh. The assault failed... partially. One of the robbers is dead, another is in prison and one or two escaped. If the assault failed, I don't see why you need me. I said it failed partially. One of the ones who escaped did so with one million dollars. You call that a failure? Officially, yes. I don't understand. That million dollars wasn't supposed to be at that branch. It was a misunderstanding between the accountant and the armoured truck company. In other words, you can't report it and so the insurance won't cover it. To tell you the truth, sir, I'd rather not have anything to do with dirty money. Why do you assume it's dirty money? Because if it weren't dirty, you'd report it and the insurance would cover it. I don't think you've understood me. Please explain. The insurance company requires us to keep track of all the cash at each branch. Because of an accounting error, this money didn't get recorded, the accountant left it for the following day. He was negligent. Report the accountant. I can't. Why not? Because he's my son. And you're sure your son isn't an accomplice of the robbers? I'd like to be able to suspect him of that, but the poor boy is so stupid he wouldn't even be capable of it. You've got to have some talent to rob a bank. If you say so... What do you want me to do? I need to find that robber and, if possible, the money. The essential thing here is that my son never comes under suspicion. What do we know about the robber? Almost nothing. And the one they arrested? You can interrogate him whenever you like, but he hasn't let out a peep. What's his name? No idea. You can speak with our contact in the police department. Who is he? Deputy Superintendent Sansone. I know him well. What are you offering? Three thousand now. If you find the robber, fifty thousand and ten per cent of the money you recover. And if I don't recover anything? Too bad for you. And if I don't find him? Also, too bad for you. And how will you know that I don't just take the three thousand and do nothing. I don't, but I pride myself on being able to read a person's character, and you don't seem like somebody who would do that. Anyway, if you were a con artist, Fermín wouldn't have recommended you and, finally, Lascano, I know a little about your situation, and I don't think you are in any position to make more enemies. Wouldn't you agree?

Perro nods. Makinlay picks up the telephone and talks to his secretary. An instant later, the girl comes in, places an envelope on the desk and leaves.

This is for you. Do we have a deal? I guess so. From now on you'll communicate only with Fermín. Whatever you need or have to say, you tell him. Understood? The one who pays, makes the rules.

Fermín hands him his card, takes his arm and walks him to the door.

At the corner of 25 de Mayo and Mitre there's a café with a curved bar to sit at and drink coffee on the fly. It's empty, too late for breakfast and too early for lunch. Perro sits down, asks for a double espresso with cold milk and a croissant. While the kid is preparing the coffee he goes over to the public phone and looks through the front pages of the phone book for the central switchboard of the police department. He sticks a coin in the slot and dials.

Good morning, this is Superintendent Lascano... I'd like to speak with Deputy Superintendent Sansone, please... Thank you... Lascano. How're you doing?... As they say, only the good die young... Fine... Yes, I know... A mess, eh?... You bet... I need to see you... The guy you've got there from the bank heist... Yeah, I talked to that Lord somebody... Who is it?... Now?... Okay, if it's got to be now, I'm on my way... In about an hour... Don't mention my visit to anybody... No worries... That's fine, I'll call you when I'm almost there... Done deal... thanks... Bye.

He eats the croissant in two bites and drinks the coffee in three gulps. It hits him like a punch from Coggi the Whip who knocked out Gutiérrez in the first round. Once he's out on the street again, a shiver runs up and down his spine. He's about to walk straight into the belly of the beast. Again. He's sick of danger, but he goes anyway.

Sansone lets Lascano in through a small side door on Virrey Ceballos. Sansone is short and energetic, an unrepentant grouch, but a straight shooter. He leads him down dark, narrow, damp and empty corridors. They end up in a kind of reception room surrounded by barred doors. A beer-bellied sergeant stands up when he sees them and opens one of the doors, lets them through, then closes it behind him. He leads them to a cell door, opens it and steps aside to let them pass. They enter, and the sergeant returns to his desk. The man in the cell has his head wrapped in a bandage. When the door opens, he looks up, on guard. Perro has known him for ages; it's Dandy Benavidez, a bank robber from Miranda the Mole's gang. He's pale and in a cold sweat. He shows all the signs of having been seriously roughed up.

What happened, Dandy? I thought you retired. What's up with you, Perro? As you see, visiting my old friends in trouble. I've got a lawyer. I know, but have I ever touched you? I just want to talk. I don't have nothing to say. Who're you working with, Dandy? Mickey Mouse. Not Miranda the Mole, by any chance? Mole's in jail. Don't bullshit me, Dandy, he just got out. You don't say? I hadn't heard.

Dandy seems to be speaking in slow motion, and it seems like he's about to start to cry. He tries to hide the tremor in his hands by pressing them together, but it doesn't work. Lascano nods at Sansone and they walk out of the cell.

115

Do me a favour. What? Go to the storeroom and ask them to give you a little boric acid. What's that? It's a chemical they use to kill cockroaches. What do you want it for? If you want a canary to sing, you've got to give him his favourite birdseed. How much do you need? Not much, a handful. You're not going to poison him, are you? Not to worry.

A few minutes later Sansone returns and hands Lascano a little paper envelope filled with white powder.

Do you smoke, Sansone? Don't even mention it, I quit a year ago. How about the sergeant? Let's ask.

They take a few steps over to the officer, who's dozing at his desk.

Hey, Medina, do you smoke? Yes, sir. Do you mind showing me your pack of cigarettes?

Medina takes a pack of half-crushed Particulares out of his jacket pocket and hands it to Lascano, who empties the contents out onto the desk. The two policemen watch him, intrigued. Perro pulls out the foil, puts it aside and returns the cigarettes to the box. He shakes out the foil and brushes off all traces of tobacco with his hand. He smoothes it out on the edge of the desk, blows on it, lays it down with the foil side facing up and pours some of the boric acid into it. He folds the paper carefully, fashioning a small envelope. He thanks the sergeant, motions to the deputy superintendent and they return to the cell. Lascano sits down in front of Dandy; Sansone sits to one side and watches. The prisoner's eyes

116

are irresistibly drawn to the little envelope on the table. He squirms in his chair. Lascano opens the envelope, just enough to give him a glimpse of the white powder.

I brought you some candy. Wouldn't a snort right about now be nice, Dandy? Don't fuck with me, Lascano. I'm not. I'm making you a business proposition. What? You give me information and I give you a little blow. You give me nothing and I snort it all myself. I'm not selling out to nobody...

Dandy's entire body betrays the urgency he feels for the coke. Nothing would feel better right now than sucking that anaesthetic in through his nostrils. Lascano observes him carefully – the prisoner has eyes only for the powder – takes a shiny new banknote out of his pocket and begins to roll it into a straw. Dandy starts to get desperate as Perro takes out the card Fermín gave him at the bank and traces two equal and parallel lines of powder on the foil.

I'm not giving nobody away, understand, Perro? But Dandy, I'm not asking you to say anything. I'm just going to ask you a few questions and you're just going to answer me with your head, yes or no.

Dandy looks at him and nods. Lascano smiles.

Mole planned the whole thing, right?... Very good, Dandy, that's the way. He ran off with the money, right?... We're doing great, any minute now you'll win the lottery, but now you're going to have to make a big effort. Where's Mole hiding?... You're not going to say? Okay, watch me, I'm taking away the

*stuff, Dandy… Give me the name of a place. Haedo… A street.
I don't know. You're going to lose it. I told you everything I
know. Anything else?…*

Lascano doesn't need to know anything else and Dandy
doesn't have any more information. As Lascano stands
up, he pretends to stumble and drops the envelope.
The white powder flies through the air, falling slowly to
the ground in front of Dandy's desperate eyes. Lascano
doesn't realize he's left Fermín's card on the table.

As they walk away down the corridor, they hear Dandy's
shouts, cursing Lascano and demanding vengeance,
echoing against the walls. The noise stops the second
the sergeant goes to the cell and opens the door.

Still laughing, Sansone and Perro leave the building
together and walk down Entre Ríos toward the House
of Congress.

*Oh, before I forget, Pereyra is looking for you. Who? Pereyra.
I don't know him. He's the prosecutor in the Third Court. A
young guy. Do you know what he wants? He's working on an
old case of yours. He said the name… but I can't remember it.
Give him a call. Did you say the Third? Yeah, the Third.*

At Rivadavia, they each go their separate ways. Lascano
continues along Callao, the name Haedo still echoing
in his head. He now remembers that's where Eva's parents lived.

The envelope keeps Lascano's chest warm. Until a few
hours ago he was alone, aimless and broke. Now he has

118

three grand, a job – to find Miranda the Mole – and a desire – to find Eva. He feels that life is beginning to take a turn in the right direction, that just maybe all the setbacks and bad luck are moving to one side and a luckier season is about to begin. It's odd, but he feels optimistic, which is much easier to do when you have three grand in your pocket. But that feeling summons another, which leads him to a rather shady locale in a run-down shopping arcade on Calle Bartolomé Mitre, where you can purchase a gun, no questions asked, as long as you know how to ask for it.

16

Lascano spends the whole night compiling all the bits and pieces of information about Miranda he has stashed away in his memory. He was in charge of the investigation that led to his arrest. Mole got off with a light sentence because he's one crook who doesn't scrimp on lawyers. He's astute and intelligent but, unfortunately, devoted to crime. He's always dreamt of convincing him to work for the police. A mind like his would be an enormous boon because you have to think like a criminal if you want to capture one.

The things that matter to a man tend to remain the same, despite time and experience. And if there's one thing that matters to Miranda, it's his family. His wife and son. As far as Lascano knows, she has nothing to do with his criminal activities. She's a "native beauty", the girl next door – though not such a girl any longer – who had the misfortune to fall in love with a crook. But she's nobody's fool: several times she managed to shake off a policeman who was tailing her to get to Miranda. The son must be about twenty by now. Too bad he doesn't have any contacts to find out what the kid is up to. He remembers spending days and days watching the house, which is what he plans to do again now.

A little before dawn Lascano stations himself in the doorway of a house on Pasaje El Lazo. From there he has a good view of the front door as well as the back, which Miranda could easily come and go through. Miranda's house is silent and still. The neighbourhood slowly begins to come to life. A Falcon carrying three plainclothes cops turns the corner at Cuenca. Perro immediately recognizes one of them: it's Flores, one of the most corrupt and bloodthirsty superintendents of the Federal Police. Lascano knows that his presence there is no coincidence. Flores has the same idea he has, except Flores is not going to waste time following the son and hoping he'll lead him to Mole, as Lascano was planning to do. He'll surely take a much more expeditious route, like, for example, kidnapping him and demanding Mole in exchange. Perro's brain kicks into high gear. He starts walking away quickly while digging around in his pockets for a coin. As soon as he's out of sight of the Falcon, he jogs to Jonte. El Quitapenas is raising its metal curtain. He dashes in, rushes to find the telephone, picks up the receiver and dials information.

Please, the number for Channel Nine...

A recorded voice recites the number, one digit at a time. He hangs up, cradles the phone between his shoulder and his ear and inserts another coin into the slot, repeating the number to himself as if it were a mantra. He dials.

...The news department, please...

It seems an eternity before they answer.

Come on, come on…

It rings six or seven times, then finally a young voice answers.

Listen, there's been a shootout here in Paternal… Thousands of shots… I think there are piles of dead bodies… I'll give you the address… Write it down, 2049 Cuenca… Half a block from the corner of Cuenca and Jonte… Yes… Is there some kind of … reward?… Jorge López… That's fine, when the van gets here I'll tell them who I am… You're welcome.

He hangs up, then dials the police. A woman answers immediately. Trying to sound arrogant and intimidating, like a lordly landowner, he spits his words out like a machine gun.

Hello… This is Judge Fernández Retamar of the Second Criminal Court… Let's see, I want to report an assault occurring at this very moment at a private residence… No, I'm in the street… It's a residence… Cuenca and El Lazo… There are three men stationed outside in the alleyway in a grey Falcon… I didn't notice… They're armed… Send people immediately… I'll wait here for you… Agreed… Step on it…

Lascano returns at a fast clip to Miranda's house but keeps walking past it at least a few yards. Everything remains calm. One of the cops stands guard, next to the Falcon, the other two are still sitting inside. He sits down on the front steps of an Italian-style house. Lascano doesn't have

123

to wait long. Two squad cars, blasting their sirens, enter the alleyway in the wrong direction and two others block the other end of the street. The car doors open and twelve uniformed police officers get out, their pistols, machine guns and rifles drawn, and crouch down behind their cars. The inspector, talking through a megaphone, orders the men in Flores's car to come out with their hands up. They register a moment of shock and confusion. The order is repeated through the megaphone. Several neighbours look out their windows. The shutters over the window in Miranda's house open and Susana looks out. Flores and the other cop descend from the Falcon and slowly lift their arms over their heads. Flores shouts that they are policemen. In response, they're told to get on the ground face down. They look at each other: they have no choice but to obey. Lascano stands up. A news van from Channel Nine arrives and brakes abruptly. Susana opens the front door, looking sick with worry. A reporter walks up to her, straightening out his tie and fixing his hair. A cameraman follows behind, shooting the scene. The uniformed officers, their fingers on their triggers, cautiously approach the men on the ground. Susana walks to the corner and tries to see who the men are. A sergeant goes up to her and takes her by the arm; she shakes him off with an indignant gesture. Flores is already standing up, angrily brushing off his suit. The inspector desperately tries to explain. Lascano smiles. Susana turns on her heels and heads for her front door, where her son has appeared. Flores seems about to levitate from rage; he motions to his men; they get in the Falcon and leave. The inspector guestures to the squad cars to let him through. Relieved, the twelve policemen return to their squad cars and leave. The reporter pats his hair into place as the cameraman returns to the van and sits down in the back seat. Lascano turns to look at Miranda's house. Leaning against the door frame, Susana, still and serious, is watching him. Perro slowly crosses the street toward her.

Mrs Miranda, I am… I know exactly who you are.

Her interruption was abrupt and bitter. Lascano opens his arms in a conciliatory gesture; she starts to close the door.

Wait. What do you want, Lascano? I'm the one who organized this whole to-do. What are you saying, that I should give you a medal? Listen to me for a second, please. I'm listening. I concocted this whole thing to stop them from kidnapping you, your son or both of you. What are you talking about? I was watching your house when I saw Flores and the other two in the alley. Who's Flores? Ask your husband when you see him. Those guys are after the money Mole stole. And they wouldn't think twice about using any means to get it. And you, what's your game? You just happened to be walking through the neighbourhood? No, I'm looking for your husband. He doesn't come here, get that through your head. That's fine, please allow me to give you some advice. Is it absolutely necessary? I think so. Out with it. Leave your house for a few days, those people are very dangerous and you can be sure they'll be back. Thank you, I'll keep it in mind.

The woman shuts the door in his face. Lascano feels a sharp stab in his chest and can't breathe. He stumbles, his head knocks against the door and he falls to the ground. Susana opens the door and sees him crumpled up at her feet. Fernando looks at him, frightened, and bends down to help him up.

Are you okay?

Perro loosens his tie and feels the air beginning to flow back into his lungs. He's drenched in sweat. Susana disappears and an instant later returns with a glass of water and a wicker chair. Lascano rejects the chair and accepts the water. He takes tiny sips. His breath is still laboured but he's starting to recover.

Are you better? Yes, it's passing, I apologize. Would you like me to call a doctor? No, it's not necessary. Are you sure?

He nods. His vision has cleared up.

Don't take lightly what I told you. Those people are dangerous. It's okay, don't worry. Another thing. What? Tell your husband what happened and that I'm looking for him. He knows he'll be safe with me. If he gets in touch with me I'll tell him. Good. Do as I say, get out of here now.

17

Sitting in the chaise longue, on that small balcony he built with the wood left over from the house, and which has become the most coveted spot, Fuseli lets the *Folha de São Paulo* drop out of his hands. He takes off his reading glasses and waits for his eyes to adjust to the distance. Soon the beach comes into focus: his woman is lying on a beach towel watching little Victoria build a sand castle with Sebastião, Leila's son. The waves, the deserted islet and behind, *el mato de la serra* that ends just a few yards from the sea at a rugged path of black rocks. Rain clouds rush across the sky. The *cachoeira* roars above the road. The Brazilian *cantiga* Leila is humming in the kitchen reaches him through the window as does the scent of the palm oil she uses to make her famous *moqueca de camarão*. He thinks that life has gotten good in this place. This love he has found is not sewn with the cloth of great passion but has instead been patiently, laboriously embroidered with threads of solitude, stitched with needles of companionship and held together with hooks and eyes of *saudades*. A tolerant and peaceful love that asks no questions and makes no demands, whose roots are sunk deep in daily life, that has never pretended to be anything more than this day-to-day existence, known to be temporary without this ever creating resentment, and that always had one mission above and beyond all else: to give little Victoria the happiness that he and his woman had been denied. That said, he never stops missing Buenos Aires. It's a feeling – definitely worthy of a tango – that embarrasses him. He was never drawn to tango music, except the *tangos duros* of Discépolo, Borges's *milongas* or the *reas* sung by Rivero, but even these, he could take only in homeopathic doses. He thinks the self-congratulatory conceit of the lyrics lacks all trace of modesty. He deplores the facile sentimentalism, the cheap sensationalism and retrograde moralizing, and, to make matters even worse, these are precisely the qualities touted with such pride as its highest virtues. Now, however, he often feels a stab of nostalgia that sounds very much like a bandoneon.

News from Buenos Aires is ambiguous. Alfonsín issues an order for the military commanders to be prosecuted. That photograph of the generals in civilian court – charges against them being read out by a bureaucrat in a grey suit and a bearded young man, treated like common criminals – brought home the fact that this was the first, perhaps the only measure any government has ever taken that has made him happy. But, in the best tradition of the Radical Party, what it wrote with one hand it tried to erase with the other when it passed the Full Stop and Due Obedience laws, an attempt to give impunity to subordinates for the brutal acts they committed with their own hands. As a consequence, nobody was satisfied, neither those demanding justice nor the *carapintadas*, the military officers who'd staged an uprising against the fledgling democracy. There are constant rumours and fears of uprisings, conspiracies, bad omens. The President insists the house is in order, but he himself must have a hard time believing it. Fuseli's dreams of returning make him want to believe it to be true.

The sky bursts open, releasing a torrent of heavy rain over the jungle, the sea and the beach. His woman gets up, calls to the children, and the three walk slowly back to the house. Here the rain is not an event to take refuge from but rather a fact of life that flows out of the sky with perfect ease. Like darkness. In the tropics night doesn't fall gently but rather pours onto the scene, like a gigantic bucketful of black water, and although it happens every day it never fails to surprise.

He looks up at the *mato*, thinks about the amount of life that swarms in among the roots of the *sambambaias*, that flies, crawls and camouflages itself, that imitates well-trained birds on the *heliconias* or that treads softly like the *oncillas* through the leaves of the *bananeiras*, as big as elephant ears. All that throbbing of pure animality, that urgency to live and reproduce, to kill and die, the entire framework of instincts, scents that mark out territories, eyes like beams, sweet or frenetic howling. All that restiveness drenched with rain. This hot land teeming with thousands of sounds, where our simian ancestors still swing from the branches that, according to Fuseli, we never should have left.

Return. To where? To what? If he returns he'll have to deal with getting a job. He has a difficult time imagining himself standing in front of a dissecting table, poking around inside cadavers to find the key to their demise, clues that would lead to a possible culprit or free an innocent suspect. Here, he has carved out a niche for himself, a place the locals have generously made available to him. Patients of all kinds come to his clinic, for he is the only doctor in a town without a hospital. In this place he has discovered the joys and the sorrows of working with bodies that are still alive. His work as a coroner was, in many ways, more relaxing. All he had to do was find out what the cadaver was trying to tell him before throwing it away. A dead body is nothing but a bunch of information to investigate, decode, order, systemize and record, but the subject himself is no longer anybody. It has no hopes, neither suffers nor desires anything, it has become an object, a thing already past its due date that is humbly initiating its process of decomposition, its return to the biosphere. It can be examined, studied, packed up and sent off to those who decide where it will go. His interaction with that dead flesh carries no commitment, responsibility or consequences, because its future is already beyond the realm of science. Because the dead force us to face our condition as beings subject to the laws of nature and our powerlessness over death, we are always so quick to hide them away in tombs, mausoleums and graves. They show us what we prefer not to see. The living, on the other hand, demand certainty; they want to be told that the inevitable moment to relinquish their suit of skin and bones has not yet arrived. They desire, feel, suffer; they place their fear, despair and pain, as well as their hopes, at their doctor's feet; they make him the repository of secrets that will cure them or at least bring some relief. Hope is a fundamental component of the healing process, hence a doctor must act as if he knows, communicate confidence, give comfort and strength to fight against illness, even though the fact is that what he knows is a mere grain of sand in the vast desert of what he doesn't.

This place is life, whereas Buenos Aires, for him and many others, is impregnated, contaminated with horror and death. His son is buried there – a wound that never heals or stops hurting. Lascano, his best friend, is there, lying in the street, gunned down like an animal by a military death squad. Through its cobbled streets and paved avenues echo the shouts of the tortured, the murdered, the young people thrown from aeroplanes into the sea and the cries of fathers, mothers, friends and lovers who will forever be missed. Return? To what? To whom? The murderers still walk around, enjoying their freedom and good health. When he thinks about his city, it seems like a place of perennial night, and its name, Buenos Aires, like a cruel joke.

18

As he makes his way down Callao toward Corrientes, Lascano thinks that the morning in 1536 when Pedro de Mendoza disembarked here must have been a morning like this one: its diaphanous sky, the temperature sweetly hovering around twenty-three degrees and a fresh and invigorating breeze explain why the spot was named Santa María de los Buenos Aires.

He crosses the avenue, preferring to walk along the plaza side of the street, where a group of men and women are practising Tai Chi. One of the young women, from the back, reminds him of Eva. He has a sensation of vertigo, a mingling of desires and fears. He also feels the urgent need to be held in someone's arms. He sits down on a bench and observes her. She turns in slow motion, her hands seem to be floating in the air, and her body appears to have become part of the atmosphere. She bends over, as if curtsying to royalty, and stretches one arm out in front of her as she straightens out her bent leg and turns to face him. As she does so, her hair falls over her face. Another turn and again her back is to him. He knows she's not Eva but still he remains there under the Araucaria trees in the plaza watching this dance that accompanies his memories: Eva is walking across his living room, a towel loosely wrapped around her, then turns and looks him in the eyes. It embarrassed him so much that he blushed, which made her smile with pride. She had an air of helplessness even though she was, is, a wild creature. She could cry for hours in the utmost despair, wallowing in her pain only to then brush it off as if it were a pest, imbue herself with magnificent power and relieve all her sorrows in a session of deep and intense lovemaking. That woman taught him the unbreakable connection between love and death, the one we try so hard to hide between the lines of ballads and madrigals.

Weary of his longing for that love, he turns his attention back to the plaza, where the girl has stopped dancing to his memories. His weariness leads him to the certainty that love has always been, for him, something that is lost as soon as it is found. He wonders if, after all, it isn't like that for everybody. Could it be that love dies as soon as we name it, trap it, try to possess it? Could it be that love either kills us or dies? Lascano feels a cry, a howl, a groan of pain lodged in his chest and squeezing his heart, trying but unable to pour out like lava flowing from an erupting volcano until it fills the skies with ash, darkening the Earth forever. The death of his parents when he was a child; Marisa, his wife, dying at the very moment they were most deeply in love; and Eva, her double, whom he loved briefly but with such intensity, and who was now lost somewhere in the world. He longs to find her but is also afraid. Who is she now, after all that has happened? Did she give birth to that child who wasn't Lascano's but might as well have been?

A gust of wind blows through the plaza and brings him back to the present. The Tai Chi practitioners gather their belongings and stand around chatting calmly. Perro stands up and crosses the plaza diagonally toward the service station. In front of Pizzurno Palace a crowd of men and women, dressed in white overalls, are protesting, demanding a raise, waving placards and making a lot of noise. He has allowed himself these moments of sorrow, a brief respite from the tasks in front of him. He has to find Miranda the Mole so he can make the money he needs to find Eva. He remembers her mentioning Brazil, Bahia to be more precise. But the map he looked at showed that, contrary to what he thought, Bahia is not a city but rather a province, and not a small one at that. His search will not be simple and he needs more facts to go on. He must find her parents. Eva talked to him about her childhood in Haedo… or might he have fabricated that memory out of his own desire and what Dandy told him about Miranda? He knows it won't be easy to find Miranda or Eva's parents, whether they are in Haedo or elsewhere. But they are the only leads he has.

At the foot of the stairs in front of the Palace of Justice a group of young women are dressed in caps and gowns and wearing mortarboards. They are handing out circulars for an information technology course for lawyers. Once in the foyer he consults his watch and sees that he is early. He turns down the corridor toward Lavalle and descends the narrow staircase to the basement, where the coroner's office is located. A sixty-something-year-old man sits at the reception desk; he is lively and talkative and chews gum and bobs his head up and down like a woodpecker. Lascano stands right in front of him and puts on his best moronic – *boludo* – face.

Good morning. May I help you? I'm looking for Dr Fuseli.

As if he had said the magic word, the Woodpecker stops chewing, glues on him a questioning stare and lowers his voice.

Who wants him?

Lascano feels like the world has stopped turning. Is his friend here?

An old friend of his. What's this old friend's name? Lascano. I knew it was you. Don't say another word. Meet me at six at La Giralda, right around the corner. I know where it is. See you there.

The man's head starts bobbing again, as if Lascano weren't there. Perro understands it's time to leave; he does an about-face and climbs back up the staircase he just came down. He returns to the elevator and gets in the queue. When Prosecutor Pereyra called, he said he wanted to talk to him about the Biterman case. He was taken aback by that young voice that spoke to him with such familiarity, and to learn that someone had resurrected the case Perro had investigated and which had almost cost him his life. Biterman, a moneylender, had been killed by Pérez Lastra, a poseur who'd fallen on hard times and owed Biterman a lot of money. The moneylender's own brother was an accomplice. The body was dumped in an abandoned field next to the bodies of some young folks who'd been summarily executed by a death squad commanded by a friend of Lastra's, Major Giribaldi. But when

Lascano took the lid off, the military creep had his friend and Biterman's brother killed, and while they were at it, Lastra's wife and several other witnesses who just happened to be in the wrong place at the wrong time. Most likely, Lascano thought, Pereyra wanted to prosecute Giribaldi for his involvement in those murders. Much of the evidence had disappeared and, best case, though improbable, he might get a short sentence for collusion and obstruction of justice. In the end, all they'd be able to pin on Giribaldi was the help he gave Lastra to dispose of the body; at the time it was impossible to hold that gang of brutal killers he commanded accountable for anything.

When Lascano walks into the prosecutor's office, Pereyra is giving instructions to a young woman with long straight hair wearing what look to him like party clothes. The young man greets him with a friendly gesture, and Lascano can't help but notice how much things have changed. These offices used to be inhabited by taciturn, musty old bureaucrats, dressed invariably in grey or brown. Now, the old farts are retiring, making way for these eager and multicoloured youths. He wonders if the change is a positive one. The prosecutor himself looks like a kid, or maybe Lascano's just gotten old. As if he could hear him thinking, Pereyra looks up and straight at him. That's when Lascano realizes he's seen this kid before, though he can't remember where. Pereyra says goodbye to the girl and doesn't deprive himself of watching – a worthwhile activity – as she leaves. When he realizes that Lascano has caught him in the act, he raises his eyebrows in a show of innocence, complicity and regret. Lascano likes this guy.

*How're you doing, Superintendent? I'm no longer a superinten-
dent. That depends, as far as I know they haven't let you go,
seems there was simply a problem with your file, it got lost and
a lot of people on the force still think you're dead. Whatever,
I'm not active. That's something we might be able to fix. I don't
know if that's a good idea, the last one who tried is pushing up
daisies. Turcheli? I see you are well informed. Sorry for asking,
but have we met before? We've seen each other. Where? You're
young, and I've been out of the loop for a while. I worked in
Marraco's court...*

In a flash the face he's looking at gets superimposed
on the face of that young pup who was working as a
clerk for Judge Marraco when he was investigating the
Biterman case.

*That kid sure has done well. Not bad. Do you remember the
Biterman case? Do I remember it? A day doesn't go by that I
don't think about it. It almost cost me my life, among other
things, and for what? Nothing ever came of it. Do you know
what happened? No idea. When you brought that envelope with
the evidence to Marraco, he had it sent on directly to Giribaldi.
I'm not surprised, I always knew he was an brown-noser. I
always thought that deep down he liked the military. He told
me to take it to Giribaldi. So? So, I did, I gave it to Giribaldi,
but not before I made and kept a copy. Did you ever find the
murder weapon? Unfortunately not, it was auctioned off by the
Banco de Préstamos. We never found the buyer, somebody from
Córdoba or Tucumán. So what now? I want to arrest Giribaldi
for the murder of a civilian. I don't think you'll get very far,
Giribaldi didn't kill Biterman, he was just Lastra's accomplice,
and even that will be difficult to prove. All the witnesses are*

dead. All except one: you. I don't think you have a very strong case. I agree, but I have another motive. What's that? Giribaldi played an important role in the death squads. He knows a lot about various issues I'm investigating. Like what? Basically, the disappeared and their children. And you think that if you press him on the Biterman case, you'll get him to talk? What, you don't think so? I think it won't be easy, but it's worth a try. That's the idea. Can I count on you? For what? First of all, to testify in the Biterman case. No problem. And second? I'm going to arrest him for his involvement in the case. With your testimony, the judge will issue a warrant. What else? It would be important to have you there when I arrest him. I want Giribaldi to think the sky is falling, and when he sees you, that's exactly what he'll think. And me, what do I get out of this? Justice, Lascano, justice. Oh, that little word… anyway, count me in. When's it going to happen? Soon, I'll let you know.

At six o'clock on the dot, Lascano walks up to La Giralda. Just as he's about to enter, he sees the man he came to meet leaning against the newspaper kiosk, smoking a cigarette. He goes up to him, making an enormous effort not to ask him for one.

Well, here I am, what have you got to tell me about Fuseli? I don't know why I'm doing this. Fuseli was always kind to me, he always treated me right and he helped me whenever he could. Do you know where he is? To tell the truth, no, I don't. Well, you asked me here, and now you're being so mysterious, you must have something to tell me. Look, Lascano, Fuseli split. Oh. Some soldiers came for him, seems he was mixed up with some subversives because… As if that mattered. What? Nothing, nothing, go on. Well, the thing is, the same day they came for him he called me on the phone. Go on. He told me that if you ever showed up, I should give you the keys to his house... My wife cleaned the house for him... Once a week... I understand... Well, here are the keys. But please, don't tell anybody I had them. Don't worry. I am worried, I don't want any trouble. It's okay, thank you. Another thing. What? Fuseli left without paying my wife, because she kept going to clean after he left. Okay, in a few days I'll stop by the courthouse and give you the money.

Fuseli's place is on the corner of Agüero and Córdoba, a small one-room apartment on an enormous rooftop terrace. He opens the door and gets a blast of a damp and musty odour. It's neat and clean and quiet. A film of dust has left a uniform greyish patina over every object and horizontal surface. He walks across the room and opens the French doors leading onto the terrace. He goes out. The sky is cold, smooth and bright. This is where he and his friend last talked. This is where Fuseli explained his theory about stars and ghosts. He said that many of the stars we see shining in the sky actually burnt out millions of years ago and that what we see now is the light still travelling through space. He said that people also emit radiation. And that, after they die, those waves can still reach the living, like the light from dead stars, and that's what ghosts are. Lascano shakes his head and a pained smile appears on his face. Fuseli would always pontificate when he smoked pot. He'd go on and on with the wackiest ideas as if they were deep revelations, vastly important insights nobody could afford not to know, truths far and away above daily miseries and petty sorrows. *He made you feel like a microbe, but a marvellous and unique microbe.* The cantina that used to be on Agüero is gone; it was an awful place, but Fuseli, a gourmet of sorts, inexplicably liked it. *Come on, let's go to the cantina where you eat crap and it's expensive and they treat you like shit.* He looks back inside the apartment. His footsteps have left an imprint on the dust on the floor. They are perfect footprints in which you can read the brand and even count the lines on the bottoms of his shoes. Perro figures you should always examine your own footsteps that carried you to this particular present, this exact situation, whatever it may be, fortunate or dreadful, joyous or sorrowful. Then you should ask yourself: how do I feel? The word that takes shape in his head is: abandoned. A shiver runs up and down Lascano's spine. He goes back inside the apartment. He looks around. The four bookshelves are full of books and photographs. Fuseli's son is smiling out of a black frame, leaning his head a little to one side and holding a green ball with rough outlines of the continents. He, Lascano, appears in another photo, laughing, sitting and eating with Fuseli and a group of men from the force in a cantina in La Boca. He contemplates those youthful faces, still not brushed by the wings of death, by the corrosive breath of lasting sorrow. He picks up one corner of the quilt over the bed; in one quick movement, he shakes it and lets it fall on the floor, raising a cloud of dust that falls with it, but in slow motion. He lies down on the bed and stares at the ceiling. He's sick and tired of feeling so alienated, so alone, of listening to his own laments. Sick of it and angry, and the anger fills him with renewed energy, and he decides that the time has come to look for Eva. This is his version of Fuseli's theory about stars and ghosts: nobody disappears without leaving a trace,

141

a footprint. Perhaps in this very apartment he'll be able to find a clue to his friend's whereabouts, but first, he decides, he'll pursue every other possibility, because he feels a certain reticence about looking through his things, dissecting his intimacy, digging into his nooks and crannies, meddling in his hidden sorrows and joys, discovering his secret pleasures, uncovering those things he chose not to share with him.

19

Lascano looks out the train window on the way to Haedo and tries to remember the address he read so long ago in Eva's police file. But no matter how hard he tries, he can't summon up the name of the street he feels he has on the tip of his tongue. With only the name of a neighbourhood and the unreliable memories of their conversations, he has decided to go and look for her parents. He knows the family owns a shoe shop near the station. He got on the train with the hope of catching a whiff of either his lost love or the fugitive. He doesn't even wonder which he'd choose if he could. He knows that in a battle between reason and passion, passion always triumphs.

He gets off the train and enters a bar, steps up to the counter and orders a *café cortado* from a young man who has an astonishing likeness to Popeye. He grinds the coffee, loads the basket, packs it in, adjusts the handle of the spout and presses the button, moving both hands at full speed to do an array of things simultaneously and with astonishing precision. The coffee tastes horrible.

Hey, kid, is there a good shoe store around here? I think there's one past the station, down Moreno.

El Perro walks through the station at the very moment two trains are arriving. The one from the centre spews out a crowd that hurries off the platform to jostle for a good place in one of the interminable queues for the buses. Perpendicular to the station, on the same axis as the waiting room, an array of awnings along the main street shamelessly compete with each other to call attention to themselves. He walks slowly down the sidewalk, made narrower by the rear ends of cars parked at a forty-five degree angle. The shop windows are stuffed with imported garbage. Lascano looks at the shops on both sides of the street, still trying to remember the address he read in the file. There was something unusual that should have helped him remember, but what was it? Ahead of him, a barefoot kid lets out a piercing shout. The greengrocer turns to look while behind him the kid's six-year-old accomplice pockets four mandarins and takes off running. Lascano watches him run by, and his lips curl into a sad smile; he remembers a phrase he heard he doesn't know where about love being a stolen fruit.

When he gets to the second block he sees it. The shop is shut and looks abandoned, but the sign is still there: in a pretentious gold-plated old-English font it proclaims: "*Zapatería Napolitano – Calzado fino para damas, caballeros y niños.*" Then, the name of the street pops into his head: Nápoles. That was the peculiarity: the Napolitano family lives on Nápoles Street.

He's in luck: the street is only two blocks long, but has about fifty buildings. He rules out the two apartment buildings, one three storeys high, the other four. Eva always spoke about a house. Didn't she also mention a front garden with roses or is that getting mixed up in his head with Marisa's family home in San Miguel? He walks up one block along one side of the street, then down it along the other. Only three houses have front yards. One has been changed into a car park for an impeccable red Renault 12. He stops in the middle of the second block to look at a one-storey house set about twelve feet back from the sidewalk. That area, which could have once been a garden, is now covered with a slab of smooth ochre-coloured cement. The facade is made of a material that looks like brick at first glance. Lascano notices a woman looking at him through the kitchen window. He crosses the street. The woman disappears. As he approaches the gate, he sees it: a quartzite stone etched with two names – Eva and Estefanía – their initials interwoven. He has found her. He rings the bell on the gate. From inside the house he hears sharp and hysterical barking and the sound of a television with the volume turned up too high. Nobody comes to the door, but Lascano suspects that the woman who was in the kitchen is now standing right behind it. It's as if he can see her twisting a rag in her hands, scared to death, unable to decide whether or not to answer. He rings again, this time holding the bell longer. The door slowly opens a crack. The woman peeks out, the chain splitting her face in two.

Yes? Good afternoon, is this home of the Napolitano family? Yes. Are you Mrs Napolitano? Yes, what can I do for you? I'm an old friend of Eva's.

The door slams shut. The dog starts barking frantically behind it. Lascano walks through the front gate and up to the door.

Ma'am, I need to talk to you... You have nothing to be afraid of... I am a friend... Please... What do you want? To talk. Who are you? My last name is Lascano...

Silence. The door opens slowly but, this time, all the way. A tall woman with grey hair appears from the shadowy interior of the house; Lascano knows that he's seen those eyes before. They are Eva's eyes.

Oh, it's you, I thought you were dead. No, I'm still alive. Come in. Thank you, Ma'am. You can call me Beba.

The little dog is a mutt, something like a cross between a poodle and a motor scooter. He nervously sniffs Lascano's shoes and in one quick movement wraps his front legs around Lascano's ankles and frenetically begins to hump him. Beba threatens to hit him with the dishcloth she has in her hand. The animal backs off a few steps, then stands watching them with nervous eyes. He remains quiet, but his entire being is aching to bark, lying in wait for his mistress to get even momentarily distracted so he can attack that leg again. With another stern command from Beba, he reluctantly creeps off to a wicker basket, where he remains, fully alert. The living room is in semi-darkness.

The house is clean and neat, but a cloud of foreboding hangs in the air and casts a dark shadow. Sitting in front of the television set in a flowered armchair and wearing pyjamas, the cathode rays casting his face in a ghostly light, Eva's father is staring blankly at the screen. His moist, partially open lips make him look perplexed. He has given no sign of noticing Lascano's presence, nor has he moved a muscle; it appears he does not even blink.

Have a seat, Lascano. Would you like some maté? Yes, thank you.

Perro looks at her. Her face looks weary, every one of her movements ending in an odd flourish of resigned indignation. She is a tall woman, graceful and shapely. She turns and catches Lascano looking at her the way a man looks at a woman's body. Her eyes glow with a sudden and evanescent flame that brings Eva to him in one fell swoop. She has those same bright green eyes whose irises seem to be spinning when they turn on you. She gives him a half smile as she hands him the maté and sits down in front of him, still holding the dishcloth.

Thank you. You're welcome. How can I help you, Lascano? I want to find Eva.

Beba jumps to her feet and slams the dishcloth against the table as if she were swatting an imaginary fly. She turns her back on him, walks over to the kitchen sink, turns back around and leans against the counter. Lascano keeps his eyes down. He knows that a broadside is coming and he expects a heavy verbal assault to follow up the daggers in her eyes. The heat suddenly feels suffocating.

Look here, Lascano. You entered through that door where a ter-
rible misfortune also entered. Actually it was Eva, my eldest, who
led misfortune in here by the hand. She's the one who brought
those ideas home from the university. Eva had a sister, did you
know that? I did. Estefanía. She was younger. Anyway, when
they came to get Eva, they took Estefanía. Do you understand?
I do. That night, my husband tried to stop those animals from
taking our daughter. They beat him to a pulp. Look what they
did to him, the poor man. He was a good-looking man and we
had the best shoe store in all of Haedo. What am I saying? In
the whole west end of the city. People came from Barrio Norte to
buy here. We had everything we needed. We worked hard and
earned an honourable living. Eva is now far away. Estefanía...
disappeared... I can't leave this house because I have to take care
of this wreck of the man I love. Do you understand me? Yes, I do.
No, no you don't! You come here asking for help. You say you
want to find Eva. Everybody wants something. Everybody has
somebody to ask for help. I don't have anybody. My life has been
reduced to taking care of Roberto until the day he dies. And then
what, Lascano, then what?!... Don't say anything. Then I'll
put a bullet through my head, though I don't even have a gun.
That's my world, the world I live in. And you come here to ask me
for help to find Eva. And me, Lascano, who do I ask for help?...

Heavy tears fall from Beba's eyes; she shows more anger
than sorrow, the pain having crystallized over the years,
become deeper, more and more compressed and bitter.
Lascano knows that feeling all too well, that sensation of
having nothing to live for, that screen falling in front of
your eyes that makes the world, even the breath you're
about to take, appear meaningless, and he can't help
wondering: what sustains this woman, how does she

148

maintain her sanity, what can she hope for from life? Lascano realizes that only by asking the right question will he hear the answer that's struggling to find its way out of her soul and into the light.

You're absolutely right, Beba. Please forgive me. Don't ask me to forgive you. I've got nothing to forgive you for. How can I help you, Beba? You want to help me? Yes, I do. You really want to help me? Yes, I really want to help you. Estefanía was six months pregnant when they took her. I know her child was born and that it's a boy. How do you know? Someone called me. They told me they saw her at a detention centre in Martínez, that she was taken to a hospital to give birth. Then they brought her back and a month later they took the boy and transferred her. Don't look at me like that, I know what it means to transfer someone.

Lascano looks at her and remains silent. The cries Beba holds back cast a shadow where the screams from the torture chambers echo.

You can't imagine what it's like to live day in and day out, night after night knowing that the monsters who tortured and killed my daughter are the same ones who live with my grandson, feed him, raise him... There's nothing any human being could have done to deserve that. Just thinking about it makes my blood boil, Lascano, it makes me want to make them suffer as I have, but then I think, I don't deserve to end up being like them. I try not to think, try not to drive myself mad. The only thing keeping me alive is the hope of finding my grandson. Do you understand me? I understand. Okay. Well... Nothing. There's nothing to say. Now I want you to go. I want to cry and I want to be alone to cry.

20

The Duchess got in touch with Gelser and told him she needed to see Miranda. Miranda was so eager to see her he arrived an hour early for the appointment Gelser set up.

Perro walks the six blocks from the Napolitanos' house to the main street. At the corner, Topolino Pizzeria is bathed in an aquamarine light. He stops for a minute to contemplate the scene on this suburban street corner, a scene that looks like it was lifted right out of *Buenos Aires en Camiseta*, Calé's satirical comic book about the city's frazzled denizens. The restaurant is packed with families, a swarm of children who think the world exists for their amusement, and who are constantly on the verge of knocking over glasses and creating other kinds of havoc. All the tables are full, and the counter as well. The people ordering pizzas or slices to go hover around the cash register, agitated and impatient. The waiters, carrying trays laden with bottles, glasses, carafes of cheap house wine and sodas manoeuvre around and through the crowds and the tables in a prodigious balancing act that acrobats of the Moscow State Circus would admire. Then he sees him: his hair has been dyed yellow, he's grown a moustache and he's wearing fake prescription eyeglasses, but it's him. Dandy didn't lie. Mole is sitting at a table smack in the middle of the room, and he's alone. Lascano takes one step back and watches him from behind the window just as the waiter brings him a large half-cheese-half-*fugazza* pizza and a bottle of Quilmes beer. He slips into the restaurant behind Mole and sneaks over to the public phone booth. The phone is broken. He goes to the cash register and asks to borrow the phone. He dials the number of the switchboard.

This is Superintendent Lascano... Connect me to the Haedo station... Give me the number then... Who's in charge there?... Thanks, kid...

He hangs up, mumbling a curse. If at all possible, he'd rather avoid talking to Roberti. He tries to remember the name of the cadet he met at shooting practice, but his name seems to have vanished from his memory. The kid, who had only a few months left before graduating, had impressed him as being very serious. He seemed to take being a policeman very much to heart, and Lascano couldn't help worrying about him, about how disappointed he'd be once he fully entered that world. He'd seen it too many times: these kids enter the academy full of ideals and end up turning into hopeless scum. That particular kid had sought him out several times to ask for advice about problems that had come up in the department, and Lascano had given it freely, being careful not to shatter his illusions but, at the same time, not shielding him from reality. He thought the kid should know that he wasn't joining a kindergarten, and that the police force was riddled with danger zones. The last time Lascano saw him, he told him he'd been assigned as a clerk in the Haedo station. But what the hell was his name? He gives up trying to remember and dials the number. The moment someone picks up the phone, the name pops into his head. He speaks, his eyes never straying from Mole.

May I please speak to Maldonado... How're you doing, kid? Lascano here... Remember me?... It's been a long time... Listen, I need a favour, tonight... but I don't want anybody at the station to find out, especially not Roberti... You up for it?... Listen, I have located a very dangerous suspect, and I want to arrest him... It's a public place and I think I'll be able to do it without problems... What I need is for you to come and give me some backup and keep him under lock and key until tomorrow... How soon can you be here?... At the pizzeria on Gaona and Las Flores... You can't make it sooner?... That's fine. I'll figure out how to keep him here... You have a car?... Bring it... Okay, be quick.

Miranda is eating his pizza with his hands, placing one slice of mozzarella face down on another of *fugazza*. Perro eats it the same way. He takes his gun out of his belt and puts it in the pocket of his overcoat, without relaxing his grip. He waits. Down the narrow aisle that leads to Miranda's table a fat woman is dragging a kicking-and-screaming six-year-old piglet to the bathroom; you'd think she was leading him to the slaughterhouse. When the way is clear, he covers the distance in three long strides and sits down in front of his prey. He takes the gun out of his pocket under the table and points it straight at him. Mole has frozen, his sandwich poised halfway to his mouth.

*Steady as she goes, Mole. We don't want to kick up a fuss.
I've got one pointing at you under the table and there are three
more surrounding you. Did you really have to ruin my dinner?
Couldn't you have waited for me at the door? Keep your hands
still. Don't worry, I know when the game's up, I'm not about to
do anything. But can I finish my pizza? Go right ahead. You
want some? No, thank you. You don't mind if I take the knife
away from you, do you? No problem, anyway I eat with my
hands. Are you armed? I'm never armed, Lascano, you know
that. The three guards your gang shot the other night wouldn't
agree. What three guards? The armoured car in Villa Adelina.
I have no idea what you're talking about. The armoured car
you attacked the other night, don't play dumb. I had nothing
to do with that. Oh, really? Just so you know what's what,
there are three dead bodies who'll point their fingers straight at
you. In Chorizo's zone, right? I think so. Now I get it. What?
They're framing me. You know very well my gang got scattered
after the last job. Dandy's in jail, and they must be putting the
screws on him, but good. The others are probably trying to find
a dung heap to hide in. And Bangs? Bit the dust, hit by a car
while he was running away. Fucking shit. At least he didn't
have a family. And you? Managed to disappear till now. Yeah,
with a cool million. Really, you don't say. But I'm sure we can
come to some kind of understanding. You know me, Mole, no
understandings. You hand over the dough to me, I return it to
the bank and I put in a good word for you with the judge. You
must think I'm some kind of idiot, Lascano. What's in it for
you? Money. And me, what am I offering you? Dirty money. If
the banker gives it to me, it's clean. Yeah, as clean as the urinal
at Retiro station. I'll give you double. Don't waste your breath,
Mole, there's not a chance in a million. Well, too bad, then,
'cause I'll need every penny of it for my family and to pay the*

lawyers, especially if Chorizo wants to lay those corpses on me. Damn right, I'm going to need a whole shitload of the stuff.

Mole finishes chewing. Impatiently, he wipes his mouth with the paper napkin and starts to fumble in his pockets. Lascano cocks his pistol. Miranda hears the unmistakable "clack" of the hammer.

Calm down, I'm just looking for a cigarette. Okay. No, it's not okay, I'm all out. Have you got any? I quit. You really didn't do the armoured-car job? Look, Lascano, I've never killed anybody and I'm going to tell you why, even though you already know, otherwise you wouldn't have chosen this place full of families and kids to arrest me. You know I'm not going to do anything that'll put them in danger. I'm a big boy now and I've already served my time. In fact, I've wasted my life. I missed out on being with my son, watching him grow up, taking him to school and all that stuff. My wife has put up with everything, but she's no spring chicken either. The truth is, I'm sick of the whole bloody thing. You know what I dream of? No, what do you dream of, Mole? My grandchildren. You're going to make me cry; ever since you became a blond, you are so sensitive. I'm serious, Perro, I imagine taking my little two-year-old out on his first walk around the neighbourhood. I can see myself a few steps behind him, keeping an eye on him from just the right distance, watching how he moves, how he reacts to things he finds along the way, teaching him how to walk, educating him. Not to be a thug, but not a wimp either. You understand? I understand. And what I don't want is for somebody to pop up behind me and put two bullets in my neck. You know what I mean? It would be a bad lesson for the kid, don't you think? Very moving, Mole, but the slammer is what's in store for you now. And then you get to go collect from the banker. To each his own. You want to tell me the difference between me, the bank robber, paying you to let me go, or the banker-robber paying you for bringing me in? Very simple, nobody's going to come after me for the money I get from the banker-robber, but they will for yours. But mine'll be double, it's a better deal and nobody's the wiser. But I'm not a businessman, Mole, I see things differently. What I don't understand, Lascano, is how you can be so intelligent and so stupid at the same time. There are many things in nature that are difficult to understand.

Lascano sees Maldonado entering behind Mole and he nods to him. He looks at the check the waiter has put in the glass with the napkins and slips in a few bills behind it.

It's on me, Mole. But you're paying on credit, Perro, and that's never a good idea. Maldonado, you go behind and I'll be in front. If he does anything smart, shoot him, understood? Understood. We'll leave by the side door. Where's the car? About thirty feet down the street. Let's go.

They step into the street, leaving behind the din of the restaurant. The cold breeze swirls around them. Maldonado stands behind Mole, watchful, holding his forty-five and looks at Lascano, waiting for instructions. But Miranda's the one who does the talking.

So, you had me surrounded, did you? And I believed you, hands down, Perro, you won that round.

Lascano smiles. Mole looks around, as if trying to find a way to escape but knowing he won't find one. At any moment it's going to start to rain. There's a cigarette stand across the street.

How about you let me buy some smokes? I'm going to need company where I'm going. I'll buy them for you, what's your poison? American, any brand.

Lascano motions to Maldonado. He takes out a pair of handcuffs and Mole puts his hands behind his back to let him put them on. They walk to the car. Lascano tells him to sit in front. Maldonado stands two yards away from the car and keeps his eyes glued on Mole. Perro crosses the street and buys three packs of Marlboro and a disposable lighter. He returns. Maldonado waits until Lascano sits down behind Miranda, then gets into the driver's seat. Because of the discomfort of the handcuffs, Mole sits crooked in the front seat.

Miranda asks permission to smoke. Lascano removes the cellophane, opens the pack, takes out a Marlboro and lights it, experiencing a powerful déjà vu. Resisting a mighty desire to inhale the smoke, he places the cigarette between Mole's lips. Miranda breathes in deeply; when he exhales, the car fills with smoke, sinking Lascano into memories of his former life.

Hey, guys, you know what I like to do more than anything else in the whole world?… Give money away. That's 'cause you're a jerk, Mole. Refined folks say it's in bad taste to give money away. Refined folks don't say that, the rich do. Because the rich don't like freedom. Is that so? No, Perro, when you give someone money, you're giving them freedom. How's that? Yeah, the freedom to choose, which is the only real freedom we have. Wow, that's really interesting. Obviously, when someone gives you cash, they're giving you the freedom to decide the what, the who and the where to spend it. Any other gift, they're also giving you a purpose, a task to carry out. You are obliged to use it, take care of it, keep it. When you give an object as a gift, you're also giving a prohibition: that they can't give it to anybody else. Objects are a constant reminder that you are indebted to the person who gave it to you. An object is almost like a curse. But cash isn't like that.

Lascano remains quiet, listening to him with half a smile. Maldonado looks at him in the rearview mirror.

You hear that, kid, now he wants to give us a gift, a gift of cash? What's wrong with that? What's wrong is that it contradicts your very own philosophy, Miranda. Why? Because you aren't offering us this little gift for nothing, but in exchange for letting you go. So? What "so"? Wasn't a gift of money supposed to be a gift of freedom? Yes. Well, in this case the only freedom you're proposing is your own. Because we'll pay the price of giving up all the things we freely believe in. No deal, Mole, I'm sorry. I'm sorrier, believe me.

They enter the station five minutes later. Maldonado speaks briefly with the officer on guard, then leads Mole to a private cell. They don't book him; nothing gets written down. Lascano and Maldonado leave together, get in the car and drive to the train station. As Perro gets out of the car, he assures Maldonado he'll come tomorrow to pick Miranda up.

21

He wakes up late. He feels like he's been trampled by the Seventh Cavalry. The day before would have been too much for anybody: he moved out of his pension and into Fuseli's apartment; he is certain that's just what Fuseli would have wanted him to do. His encounter with Eva's parents was like a hammer blow to his head, and the *coup de grâce* was catching Mole off guard, so to speak. Now he hasn't a moment to lose; a guy like Miranda has more tricks up his sleeve than a card shark. He checks the time then dials Pereyra. He wants to get an arrest warrant so he can bring Miranda from the Haedo station to the court-house. Once he's delivered him signed and sealed, he can go and get his money from Fermín. He has very little hope of finding any of the stolen money; in fact, he has no hope at all. He gets Pereyra's answering machine. He leaves a message, asking him to get in touch as soon as possible.

Vanina spends the twenty minutes Marcelo is late putting up stoically with the gaping stares of the lawyers who fill the Usía Café. She had planned to carry out this little conversation in the kindest, most loving way possible, but waiting for him and being drooled over have soured her mood. A few days earlier a man came to the university to give a class on the theory of colour. He's an architect, about forty-five years old, who stopped designing buildings and now devotes himself to the fine arts. He stands in front of the class with his dirty-blond beard, his turtleneck sweater and his Clark suede boots. She doesn't know how it happened, but she went to see him at his studio in San Telmo, to take a painting class with him, and they ended up in bed. Now she thinks she should break up with Marcelo. She's eager to be free so she can live fully this new love, discover the infinite world of art with Martín guiding her. She can't decide whether or not to tell Marcelo about him, so she decides to decide when the time comes. She looks again at her watch – half an hour is really too long – and motions to the waiter to bring her the bill. She feels relieved she doesn't have to confront the issue right away, but the relief doesn't last long: Marcelo is entering the café. His hair is mussed up and he's carrying a bundle of papers under his arm. In a split second, she feels contempt for everything this man isn't and she wishes he were.

I'm so, so sorry. You're hopeless, Marcelo. I'm really sorry. I was just about to leave. Lucky you didn't. I don't think it's lucky. What's going on, Vanina? What's going on is that I want it to end. Want what to end? Don't play dumb. Our relationship, what else? Why? Because it's not going anywhere. Is this because I got here fifteen minutes late? A half-hour. Okay, a half-hour. No, it's not. So what's going on? It's because of you, of me, of us. I don't think I can live the kind of life I want to live with you. What kind of life do you want to live? I don't know, more poetic, more artistic. You spend your life buried under piles of papers. Just look at you. You met someone else, didn't you? No.

Don't bullshit me. I swear, Marcelo, I didn't. What happened last night? Nothing. You said you'd come over and you never showed up and never called. It didn't seem to have worried you very much. I called and you didn't answer, then I called your parents. Your mother didn't know what to tell me. Here you go, acting like a prosecutor even when it's about us. No, Vanina, I was worried. Why did you call my parents' house? I just told you… Look, I need my freedom. Tell me the truth. The truth is, I don't love you any more. Are you sure? Yes, I am, and I'm sorry. There's nothing to be sorry about. We really should talk more but I have to go now. It's my fault, I was late. If you want, we can meet later. I don't know, I have a lot of studying to do. Okay. Are you okay? I don't know. Well, call me if anything comes up. I'll call you if anything comes up.

Marcelo watches her leave the café. He's sure of it: she's met somebody else. He feels wretched. Vanina is everything he's ever dreamt of in a woman.

He always believed he'd end up marrying her and having two or three kids. This was totally unexpected. He watches her cross the street and disappear into the crowd milling around the courthouse. *Is that how somebody walks out of your life?* Her lipstick has left an imprint of her lips on the coffee cup. The day begins under the pall of lost love. The sudden anticipation of all the problems he'll have to deal with at work turn his sadness into a formidable surge of ill temper and he jumps out of his chair.

The telephone starts to ring the second he enters his office. He grabs it and it slips through his fingers, falling at his feet. He picks it up, still ringing, and presses a button as if it were the trigger on an atomic bomb.

Yes… What's up Lascano?… I was about to call, I just got to my office… That's fine, we'll talk about it later, but right now, something urgent… I understand, but this can't wait… The Giribaldi thing is happening today… This afternoon… As soon as I get there I'll arrange everything and call you… Okay… No problem… Better still… Yes… we'll talk in a bit.

Perro finishes his shower. He looks at himself in the mirror. Every day he spends a few minutes contemplating that scar that decorates his chest. It's a pale island in the shape of a half moon. It still hurts if he touches it in the middle, but around the edges there's no feeling whatsoever. Once, under circumstances he can't recall, Fuseli told him that our scars are there to remind us of the past. Now, as he's getting dressed, he feels like he's about to crash headlong into that past. Soon, he'll be with Pereyra, striking fear into the heart of the man who ordered his death. The fearsome Giribaldi himself, a man mentioned over and over again by the few survivors of Coti Martínez detention centre in the report, called *Never Again*, which documented the torture, murders and disappearances carried out by the military. Famous for giving his victims lessons in morality with the cattle prod in his hand, he wrote on the wall of his torture chamber: *If you know, sing; if not, singe.* As he walks out, he dedicates a thought to all those who will leave their houses today and never return.

22

A storm darkens the afternoon. With perfect synchronicity, he walks out of the door of the building at the very moment a bolt of lightning illuminates the streets, thunder crashes and the rain pours down, rain Lascano can't help thinking must be dirty. He feels a chill, thinks these are bad omens, has a foreboding – almost a certainty – that something very grave is about to happen. He lifts the collar of his jacket and starts walking up Agüero toward Cabrera. As he gets into a cab, a wave of nausea washes over him, a taste of how he's going to feel in a few minutes when he sees Giribaldi. By the time the cab stops, the rain has turned into a veil hanging in the air, drenching the world. Two squad cars and two Falcons without number plates are parked in front of the building. Marcelo is talking to a uniformed officer and four patrolmen stand off to one side, smoking and chatting. There's tension in the air, and Lascano is not the only one who feels it. What he wouldn't give right now for a cigarette. Marcelo holds out his pale, cold hand in greeting, then takes Lascano's arm and walks through the door held open by the doorman. They are followed by the officer and one of the policemen. The doorman brings up the rear, waiting until the four men get into the elevator. When the light on the panel shows that they've reached the first floor, he picks up the intercom and presses a button.

Giribaldi is checking the cleaning supplies when the buzzer sounds. The doorman whispers to him through the intercom that the police are on their way up to his apartment. He rushes out of the kitchen, takes four long strides down the hallway and enters his office. He finds the box where he keeps his nine millimetre, takes it out, checks to make sure it is loaded, cocks it and places it in the large top drawer of his desk. The bell rings. He takes a deep breath. He walks slowly to the front door and opens it.

Yes. Good afternoon. Good afternoon. Are you Mr Leonardo Giribaldi? At your service. I am Marcelo Pereyra, Public Prosecutor for the Third Criminal Court. I have a search warrant. May we come in? Please. Is there anybody else at home? No, I'm here alone.

As if they were performing a carefully rehearsed dance routine, Giribaldi moves aside, and Marcelo and Lascano open the way for the policemen to enter the apartment. Giribaldi stares at Lascano, obviously recognizing him. Pereyra motions to Giribaldi to go in ahead, and they follow him into his office through the first doorway down the hallway. The major sits down at his desk and motions to them to have a seat in front of him. The officer appears and indicates to the prosecutor that he has searched the house and everything is under control. Marcelo carries out the legal formalities, informing Giribaldi that he is under arrest and reading him his rights. Giribaldi looks at him as if from a great distance, absolutely indifferent to his words. He looks down: through the crack of the open drawer he can see the black grip of his fearsome Glock.

Lascano has a hard time believing that this is the same man who held so many lives in the palm of his hand, who doled out so many deaths on a whim. But now, facing him, he cannot see even a trace of the confident and implacable tyrant he once was. That is a defeated man sitting behind that desk. The cruel sheen in his eyes has completely faded, and they now express nothing but insensible resentment. Nothing remains, there's nothing to wait for, no hope is left. Suddenly, he turns his eyes on Lascano, and in a harsh voice, as if he were barking orders at his troops, he interrupts Marcelo.

I recognize you. Yes, we have seen each other. You're Lascano, that traitor of a cop who was hiding a subversive. Excuse me, but you are the one under arrest. If you think this is where it ends, you've got another thing coming.

Lascano goes on high alert. He moves his hand slowly toward his shoulder holster. He can see from the look in Giribaldi's eyes that behind that calm exterior he is completely nuts. He knows that anything could happen at any moment. Marcelo starts up where he left off. Giribaldi stands up, does an about face, opens the window and returns to his chair. He smiles scornfully.

I suddenly smelt something putrid: a traitor's shit. You two probably don't smell it because you're used to it, but I find it unbearable.

Giribaldi again looks down. Here he is, Lascano of all people, coming to finish him off, put an end to the little bit of life left to him. This is the collapse, the final act. He looks up and meets Lascano's eyes. His mind is racing as it always does when he is about to go into action. He wonders, as a challenge to himself, if he'd have time to grab the gun and shoot both Lascano and Pereyra before they can defend themselves. He's not used to having doubts, but now he hesitates. He imagines the report. The nine millimetre is a loud weapon.

Giribaldi doesn't answer any of Pereyra's questions. He doesn't even hear them. He looks at him not only with resignation but also astonishment at the young man's insolence. He stands up and walks over to the window. He sees the squad cars, the Falcons and the other policemen on the street. He looks at the time. Any moment now Maisabé and Aníbal will be arriving. He sits back down at his desk, rocks back and forth in his chair and looks at Marcelo and Lascano with opaque eyes. Marcelo shows impatience, stands up and walks out of the room. He suspected this might happen. Giribaldi realizes he has gone to get the policemen so they can place him under arrest. The image of General Videla, entering the court in handcuffs like a common thief, flashes through his mind.

You got away from me, Lascano... I was lucky... Just like the rest of you: we won the war but now you're going to beat us at peace. There never was a war, Giribaldi. This peace, this "democracy", Lascano, we made it happen. The civilians stayed at home with their tails between their legs when the commies came with their bombs and their kidnappings. Don't give me that shit, Giribaldi, there's no justification for what you did. And now it's people like you, who we let live, who are going to judge us. It's our own damn fault, we should have finished the job.

Suddenly that face, that monstrous gaze of this merciless man, turns into a twisted grin of pain but also awe at what he knows he is about to do. Lascano feels a cold chill run up and down his spine. He clutches the handle of his gun. He has a moment of insight and knows for certain that they won't both come out of there alive, like in a duel scene in an old Hollywood western. Giribaldi's mind is empty and silent, but the next instant an engine explodes inside of him, his jugular vein bulges.

Here, Lascano, here's something you'll never forget...

He moves with the speed he's so good at mustering: he rises, pushes the chair back against the wall, grabs his gun, pulls it out of the box, puts the barrel in his mouth and... Lascano barely has time to draw his gun halfway out of the holster when Giribaldi flies backward, landing in his chair, his head banging against the seat back then falling forward on his chest. From his nostrils spurt two streams of blood that flow down onto his shirt; the gun drops out of his hand and his arms hang by his sides. The bullet, passing through the walls of the skull, has left the imprint of a bloody mandala on the wall behind Giribaldi – it frames his dead face, like the halo of a macabre saint. Silence. Footsteps. Pereyra bursts in, the two policemen behind him.

Holy Christ! What the hell happened? He pulled a gun and blew his brains out. I didn't have time to do anything.

Perro, still shattered by the shock, staggers out of the room. Pereyra gives an order to call the coroner. For a split second of hope, Lascano imagines that Fuseli will be the one to show up, as he has so many times in the past. He walks into the living room and collapses into a chair. On the wall in front of him hangs the pennant of the Colegio Militar, with its image of a castle chess piece surrounded by a laurel wreath. Pereyra comes up to him, sits down, takes out a pack of cigarettes and offers one to Lascano. He looks at it as if it were a lover who had jilted him. He reaches out his hand, but seconds before grabbing it he lifts his palm in a gesture of refusal. He's sweating. He stands up, walks over to the window, opens it and goes out onto the balcony. Below, standing next to the patrol car, a woman with a child is talking to the officer. He turns and enters the building. Lascano returns from the balcony. Pereyra stubs out his cigarette. Perro walks through the final cloud of smoke and inhales deeply. The apartment is full of police. The officer who was talking to the woman approaches them.

Sir, the wife and child are down below. Don't let them up, I'm going down.

Pereyra and Lascano look at each other, wondering who will be the one to tell her the news. Without exchanging a word, they decide it will be Perro, because he is older. As if being that much closer to death confers upon him more authority. They ride the elevator down in silence.

When they get to the ground floor, Marcelo opens the door and lets Lascano go out before him. Maisabé is a few yards away, standing in the street with her back to them, a policewoman on one side and the child on the other. As they start to walk toward them, the woman turns and looks at them, questioningly. Marcelo takes the child by the hand and asks him to come with him. Maisabé glues her eyes on Lascano.

Is he dead? Yes, Ma'am. You killed him? No, Ma'am, he killed himself. Do you realize what you have done?... You should have killed him... What? You must be a heretic, that's why you don't understand. Excuse me, what should I understand? You've condemned his soul. What? Suicides can't enter heaven!... I'm very sorry, Ma'am. You are not sorry and that's obvious. Forgive me. Only God can forgive you.

The woman glares at him with fury, turns her back on him and walks resolutely toward the patrol car, where a policewoman is talking to the child. Marcelo walks up to Lascano.

This sure turned out like shit. What else do you think could have happened? You're probably right. Our past always catches up with us. What are you going to do now? I'm tired, exhausted. All I want now is a bath and a bed.

Pereyra knows he's not going to get any sleep tonight. They shake hands and say goodbye. Lascano walks to the corner. For some unimaginable reason, he turns and looks at Pereyra talking to a policeman, who nods and heads to the building. Marcelo goes up to the child, talks

169

to him, then gives him his hand and they also begin to walk toward the door of the building. At that moment, the child turns around and looks at Lascano. His heart skips a beat. Those eyes! That combination of defiance and melancholy, yes, more than anything, it's the look in his eyes. Could it be? He watches him disappear behind the door, holding Marcelo's hand, and he feels beleaguered, undone. A taxi drives by, he stops it and he gets in. There's a pack of Lucky Strikes on the dash. *What the hell.* Lascano asks the driver for a cigarette, which he gives him reluctantly. He lights it and leans back in the seat. Behind him, the corner where that tragedy took place begins to drift into the past tense.

Damn!

23

Several times during the long night, Lascano is woken by the same dream. He's stark naked and walking down a narrow corridor of fog, which seems to go on forever. Suddenly, through the haze, there emerges the greyish outline of a human figure carrying a lance adorned with multicoloured precious stones. The faceless man points the lance at him and says: *If you don't do something with your life, I'll take it away from you.*

In the morning, he cuts himself near his lip while shaving; the blood spurts out. He lets it drip down his face. Contemplating himself in the mirror, he is reminded of a vampire in a B movie, the kind he'd see in the neighbourhood theatre when he was a child and when this life he is leading was still unimaginable.

He decides to go and pick up Miranda. But first he must see Pereyra to get him to expedite the order that would make Mole's detention a formal arrest.

When he gets to Marcelo's office, they tell him they don't expect him until noon. He leaves word that he will be at the Usía, the café in front of the courthouse on Tucumán. He leaves the Palace of Justice, enters the café and starts reading the paper.

He's about to finish when Marcelo arrives, sits down in front of him and orders a *café cortado*.

How was your night? It's still not over, I haven't slept a wink. You know what, Pereyra? What? I'll wager a lot of money that boy is not the Giribaldis' son. Why? I think he was stolen. Why? Didn't you notice last night, he never even looked at his so-called mother? And what's that supposed to mean? In a stressful situation, a kid'll usually look at his parents, his way of finding out what's going on. It's natural. Well, this one didn't. I didn't notice. I did. And there's something else. What? That boy looks a lot like some people I know whose grandson was taken at Coti Martínez. You really think that's him? Hell, I don't know what to think. Could just be wishful thinking that those people find him. Who are they? A family in Haedo, last name Napolitano. Tell them to call me and we'll do a DNA test. Good. I wanted to talk to you about something else, about Miranda. Who? Miranda the Mole, the bank robber…

It takes Lascano a few minutes to explain the situation. They agree they'll give the chief of the Haedo precinct credit for the arrest and that Lascano himself will be in charge of transferring him. The prosecutor tells him that he'll look the other way as far as his illegal detention of Miranda goes, but warns him that's the only irregularity he'll let slide. Lascano agrees and congratulates himself for not mentioning anything about the reward. Nor does Marcelo think to ask him his reasons for detaining him; they've already established a bond, common cause as enforcers of the law. Marcelo lends him his car and tells the driver and a policeman from the Tribunales police station to accompany Lascano to pick up Miranda. They get in the car and leave. A movie showing an endless series of moments of other people's lives passes by the car window.

In the meantime, Mole is smoking a cigarette and waiting calmly in his cell. A guard walks by. In the office next to him, Peloski, the officer in charge, comes on duty, a stack of papers under his arm. Miranda calls to the guard.

Hey, kid. What's up? Do me and yourself a favour. What? When Roberti arrives, tell him Miranda the Mole is here and that it's important. The super is going to be grateful to you. If I see him I'll tell him. Thanks.

Mole watches him walk away down the hallway and smiles. Peloski has overheard part of the conversation. He stops the guard as he walks by.

Who were you talking to? The prisoner. There's a prisoner? Maldonado brought him in yesterday afternoon. He spoke with Medina, then left him here and took off.

In a quick glance Peloski checks the log. Nobody's been booked.

What did he tell you? That when I see Roberti I should let him know that Miranda the Mole is here. He told you he was Mole? Yeah, Mole. What else did he tell you? Nothing, that Roberti would thank me. Okay. Do me a favour, go to the armoury, see if Gómez is there and send him to me. At your service, sir. We are all at God's service.

Going to and from the armoury won't take less than fifteen minutes. Plenty of time for what Peloski is planning. When the spring hinge shuts the door, he goes around the counter and walks the few steps down the row of cells until he sees Mole sitting there, smoking peacefully. Mole looks up and nods. Peloski has no further doubt: that's Miranda the Mole all right. He goes back to the counter, but first he opens the door and checks to make sure there's nobody outside in the corridor. He picks up the telephone and dials a number.

Hello, Superintendent. Peloski here... Listen. We've netted a very interesting fish here at the station... He's been prepped and is ready for the grill... I'd get here right away... I know, I know, but this one's worth the trouble... Okay... No worries... Right... I'll expect you... Make it quick.

Lascano gets out of the car and rings the doorbell. Beba opens it immediately and steps aside to let him in. When the mutt sees him, he dashes out like a wind-up dog and lies down in his basket.

Any news? Nothing much, Beba. Last night I was present at the arrest of an army major, the man who ran Coti Martínez. Oh. So? Well, it turned out pretty bad, because before we could do anything he grabbed a gun and shot himself. Why are you telling me this, Lascano? It's just that this major and his wife live with a boy they say is their son. Fortunately, the boy wasn't home when it happened, but he arrived a while later. And? I can't be sure and I don't want to raise any false hopes, Beba... But? But that boy looks a lot like you and Eva, though I might just be imagining things. I want to see him. Look, the case is in the hands of Marcelo Pereyra, a public prosecutor. I already told him about you and he's expecting you to call him. Here's the number. Thank you. You've got nothing to thank me for and I suggest you don't get your hopes up. I don't think you need to suffer any more than you already have. Let me be the judge of that. As you wish. May I ask you for something? What? A picture of Eva.

Beba walks into the back room and returns a few minutes later with an instant photograph: Eva in a bikini on a terrace with sun umbrellas above a beach. The shadow of the man who took it is falling over her lap. Suddenly overwhelmed with emotion, Lascano stuffs the photograph in his pocket.

On an impulse that surprises Beba and himself, Lascano gives her a kiss on the cheek, turns on his heels and leaves the house. Just when he's about to open the door of the car, he hears Beba calling out to him. He turns around.

Come here a minute.

Twenty minutes after Peloski's call, Roberti enters the station. If he'd come a bit sooner, he would have crossed paths with the guard who was supposed to give him Mole's message and whom Peloski had sent on a mission for the sole purpose of getting him out of the way. The officer smiles at the superintendent.

Who is it? Miranda the Mole. No kidding, who brought him in? Lascano, with Maldonado. Perro? The very same. I thought he bit the dust. He's alive and kicking. Word in the force is that

175

he's dead. He's working for himself. Did they book him? No, I'm telling you he's ready for the grill. Go see for yourself. Don't let anybody disturb us. Leave it to me, but afterwards, don't forget your poor friends.

Peloski points his finger in the direction of the cells, as if this were necessary. Roberti takes a few quick strides down the hall. When he sees Mole he slows down, then stops. He picks up a bench that's leaning against the wall and brings it up close to the bars of the cell where Mole is sitting peacefully and smoking.

Mole! How delightful to see you. You've got no idea how happy I am that you've come for a visit. How're you feeling, Roberti, old friend? Very well, Mole, very well, and I'm quite sure I'm going to feel even better very shortly. There's nothing like a man with faith. Let's see, what shall we do: we come to some kind of understanding or I book you? What about Lascano, what do we do about him? Lascano is already taken care of. How? Perro isn't with the force any more. He got involved with subversives. I thought they'd killed him, but it seems like he got away and now he's slipped back. Just one more of the benefits of democracy. That means he nabbed me for nothing, the motherfucker. He screwed you big time.

Mole sits there for a moment staring off into space, his index and middle finger holding the cigarette. He tosses the butt to the floor and crushes it. He smiles.

What were you asking me? If we should make a deal or if I should book you?

176

Lascano stops in the middle of the living room, just a few feet away from the armchair where Eva's father is sitting and staring at the television screen. Beba walks over to the wooden sideboard, opens a drawer and starts rifling through a pile of papers. For a quick instant, the man moves his blank eyes away from the TV and glues them on Lascano, who feels obligated to look at him and give him an equally blank smile. Beba closes the drawer, turns and hands Lascano a somewhat crinkled airmail envelope.

There you have it, Eva's address; she talks about you in the letter... and about herself.

Lascano hesitates, afraid of what this letter might say, but he ends up taking it, glancing at it, then stuffing it in his pocket. He feels the need, the urgent need, to leave that house as quickly as possible

Thank you, Beba, but... Don't say anything, Lascano. I wish you luck.

He nods, turns around and walks out. As he closes the door behind him he feels like he is about to faint. He inhales deeply, then exhales, then walks to his car. As the chauffeur drives him to the station he imagines what that family must have been like before it was destroyed by the death squad. Probably much like the family he always looked for, dreamt about, longed for. The one he kept believing he would find, but something always got in his way. The death of his parents, the accident that took Marisa away, Eva's precipitous escape when those military bastards ambushed him. He hopes with all his heart that Beba finds her grandson. He hopes that child can live what remains of the childhood they stole from him, stop pretending he believes the lies of the adults around him, grab a cat by the tail, play hooky at school, play with matches, be loved, cuddled, scolded – without a horrendous secret always getting in the way. The car stopping abruptly in front of the station brings him back to the here and the now.

Lascano's ride into the centre is a long, one-of-a-kind cursing session against that Goddamnmotherfucking-sonofabitchRoberti. He can't believe he let Mole go. He must have paid him off, like he tried to do to him, but Roberti took him up on it and here Lascano is, once again, in deep shit. When he finishes cursing the super-intendent, he starts on Pereyra. If he hadn't delayed him this morning, Mole wouldn't have got away. But things don't work out like that; luck is a whore who is usually fucking someone else.

24

All afternoon and well into the night, couples get in their cars and drive to the Palermo forest to do whatever it is couples do in their cars. This custom, so deeply ingrained in the inhabitants of Buenos Aires, has led to the area being called Villa Cariño – Tenderness Town. The local cops, paid off by the proprietors of the nearby bars, mind their own business. This is where Miranda the Mole has chosen to meet his wife, because this is where they used to come when they were first dating. Here he brought her proudly in his first stolen car. Here they made love for the first time.

Sitting in his one-hundred-per-cent-legal car, he listens to a cassette of Frank Sinatra while he waits for her. She must have taken the long way around, to shake off any possible tails. He trained her well. Yes, that must be why she's late. He keeps looking in the rearview and side mirrors. He catches glimpses of what's going on in the other cars: couples are drinking, kissing, fondling each other; here and there someone still needs convincing of what she'll end up doing anyway; a blonde ducks, disappearing from sight. The glories of Villa Cariño. A taxi stops on the corner. It's her. He watches her pay, get her change, get out of the taxi and look around for a sign. Miranda

switches his headlights on and off and she walks toward
him. Her hips sways back and forth, silhouetted against
the red brick wall. He watches as she approaches with
quick steps, then she gets in the car, closes the door and
without looking at him, drops her head. She's crying.

*What's wrong, my Duchess? I can't do it any more, Eduardo,
I can't. That's what's going on. But, why, Duchess? You want
to know why? Of course I do, my love. I'm going to tell you
why, but please, let me talk. Don't interrupt me. Speak, tell me
whatever you want. Okay.*

Susana looks down, takes a handkerchief out of her purse
and wipes her nose. She takes a deep breath. Miranda
leans back against the door so he can see her better,
then places his arm over the steering wheel.

*You stood me up the other night at the pizzeria. I had a problem,
I couldn't make it. I told you not to interrupt me!*

Duchess is speaking in a whisper, but it sounds like she's
shouting. Miranda bites his lips.

*I'm worried to death. What are you worried about, Duchess?
Everything, I'm worried about everything! Ever since you got
out, I've been living in a state of panic. A few days ago there
was a big commotion right outside the house, cops and television
cameras. I went out to see what was going on. I thought you had
come and they were there waiting for you. But it was something
else. So, what about it? There was someone at the door, Lascano.
Lascano? Yeah. He told me he'd arranged all that to stop them
from kidnapping us to get the money you stole. Who was going*

to kidnap you? I don't know, some cops. Lascano mentioned someone by the name of Flores. He told us we should leave the house because he said they'd definitely be back.

Susana is twisting the handkerchief in her hands, and a stifled groan escapes her lips. Miranda watches her, trying to muster his courage. She shoots him a look full of resentment.

I can't even be in my own house any more! Where are you living? At my uncle's. And Fernando? Fernando, too, I wouldn't abandon my son!

Susana lets this reproach rip like the lash of a whip. Miranda receives it like the stab of a knife in his gut.

Calm down, Duchess, please. I don't want to calm down! I'm furious and I want to be furious, don't you understand? But that's not the end of it. The other morning, when I went out shopping, I saw it. What? On the front page of the newspaper, at the stand on the corner. A full-page picture of three people lying in a pool of blood, and next to it was a picture of you and three other guys. I felt this blast of rage and sadness tearing through my chest... Carlos, the newspaper man, who's been there ever since I was so big, he was watching me, spying on me, waiting to see my reaction. All I could do was stand there, paralysed, staring at the picture, wondering if it was you lying dead on the front page? I didn't dare go and find out. Had my worst fears come true? Then Carlos, as if he knew what I was thinking, said it wasn't you, that you'd escaped. Those words broke the spell. It was as if they woke me up. I looked at Carlos and I realized how he'd aged, and seeing him I realized that I had too. He looked at me sadly, with compassion, as if to say "What can we do?" It tore at my heart. I refused the paper he offered me. I didn't want to know any details… All day every day we make little decisions, one after the other, we think that at some point it's all going to come together, start to make some kind of sense. But these decisions keep piling up, that's what our lives are made of, they make us who we are and determine what's going to happen to us. In the end, we are what happens to us. And what's happening to me is that I just want to go home and cry. And that's what I do. I throw myself face down on the bed and curse my fate, and I cry, first with rage, howling furiously like a wild animal. Then comes the pain and the sadness. The house is quiet, and I keep asking myself why the hell I married you, why the hell do I keep waiting for you? Why? Then I realize that this time you weren't the dead body on the first page of the newspaper. Not this time. I realize that maybe that's what I'm waiting for, that it be you, and I don't want to feel that, Eduardo. But that's what I've become: a widow waiting for them to bring me the corpse, for my fate to finally play itself out, and all I want is for it to end, once and for all. And I don't want that, Eduardo, not that. Forgive me, but I can't do it any more. I want to make a new life for myself and I can't wait any longer. Now again they're hunting you down, and as usual they'll find you and, if you're lucky, you'll go to prison. For how long this time? Five years, ten years, life? I've never loved… I will never love anybody like I've loved you, but I think I've earned the possibility of a tiny little piece of happiness in this life, and that's what I want, Eduardo. And with you that won't be possible. But, Duchess, you can't leave me now. I'm not leaving you, Eduardo, you left me a long time ago and you didn't even realize it.

A heavy, marital silence descends, now denser, more unbending, irremediable. He looks at her, she looks back at him and for the first time understands how different they are in every way. She has the sensation that they are no longer a man and a woman of the same species, that they never really were, they were only ever joined in some kind of unnatural symbiosis. Whatever it was that kept them together has shattered in a way that is beyond repair. They are two strangers stranded in this field of lovers. We are of the material world, she thinks, and the material world exacts its revenge. Just like when a job is shoddily done, without mindfulness or respect. A thing poorly done remains like a curse, always there to remind us of our faulty workmanship.

When Susana gets out of the car, Miranda turns off Sinatra. He feels like crying, like breaking something. He has the worst of all sensations: impotence. She's right, there's nothing he can do to make things right, to fix what he set out to destroy. She has always been loyal and faithful, and he always knew he was ruining her life, but over and over again he figured he'd pull one final job that would lift him above the fray, and then they'd be able to go to another country and live the lives of kings, and never worry about anything ever again. But that goal was as phony as a three-dollar bill. Because what Miranda really likes is to take risks. All that crap about going straight once and for all is just a ploy to justify himself. Now the time has come to pay off his debt to Duchess. He feels like his heart is crumbling inside his chest. He doesn't make the least effort to hold her back, to try to convince her, to seduce her as he has a thousand times. He stays in the car until he gets so cold he has to drive.

Two days after Duchess's goodbye, Miranda parks his car in front of her uncle's house. He doesn't have to wait long before he sees his son cross the street with a hurried step. He rolls down the window and calls out to him. The young man stops and, surprised and baffled, looks at the man in the car.

Papa?... Hey, son. Get in.

Which he does. He sits down in the passenger seat, throws his backpack in the back seat and stares straight ahead of him, in silence. At that moment he feels like he hates his father.

When did you get out? A few days ago. And you're already in trouble again. It's my style, what can I do? How is it possible that somebody of your intelligence simply doesn't get it? What should I get? Something you yourself told me when I was still a little kid. What did I tell you?... That if your main investment is your body, you're not in the right business. We say all kinds of crap... It's not funny. What isn't funny? You're not the only one in danger. The other day they tried to kidnap us. Mama told me. Yeah, she spent the whole day crying. One of the cops gave us a message to give to you. Who? Lascano. He said you should turn yourself in to him, that you'd be safer. Thanks. Leave it to me, I'll work it all out. You'd better. I want to talk, I've got something very important to tell you. I can't now. You in a hurry? Yeah, I am, in fact. Can we meet for lunch? When? Whenever you want. Tomorrow?... Where? Remember that place we used to go when I'd pick you up from school? On Luca Street? That's the one.

Fernando grabs his backpack, gets out of the car without saying goodbye and walks away. It doesn't take Miranda long to get Flores's phone number.

Flores, Miranda here... Why the hell are you fucking with my son?... You're a family man, you sonofabitch... I don't give a fuck... Okay... What do you want?... Not a cent... no more than a hundred grand... I said no... Are you nuts? With that money I can blow you and your entire family away. Take the hundred and stop busting my balls... I'm telling you, no, Flores... and don't make me lose my patience... Okay... Good... I'll take care of it... I know, Flores, it won't be the first time... Friday at the latest... No... No...

25

What the hell do you mean he wasn't there?! Just that, he wasn't there. Did he escape? He couldn't have escaped because officially he wasn't even there. They never booked him? No. What happened? Depends who was at the station. If it was Roberti, Miranda paid him off with the money from the heist. If it was Flores, Miranda is probably dead and buried after a brutal interlude. What do you think? I want to believe it was Roberti. Why? Humane reasons. Mole isn't a killer, he's just a bank robber, and an old-fashioned one at that. Seems you kind of admire him. I've always admired intelligence and Miranda is a very intelligent guy, though his methods... Too bad he doesn't use his intelligence for something worthwhile. What do you want me to tell you, Pereyra? That in a country like this one, where the government, in cahoots with the big companies, robs people of the desire to live, where a guy can spend his life busting his balls and all he gets is a pension that doesn't even pay for his morning coffee... Better to be poor and honourable, Lascano. Oh, really? So tell me, why are the prisons so full of poor people? Because they don't have money for lawyers. You're an honest bloke swimming in a sea of corruption and trying to keep your nose above the shit. Let's say, I'm a little more honest than the others, but the truth is, I don't know if it's out of conviction or cowardice. And I don't really care to find out. I just hope, Lascano, that when I'm your age, I don't think like you do. And I, Marcelo, share that hope for you, with all my heart.

Once outside, he decides to walk. He has in his pocket all the information he needs to get in touch with Eva. Juquehy... He likes that name. The problem now is where the money will come from to get there. Mole has vanished and he's losing steam; he couldn't care less about anything besides finding Eva and seeing if there is any possibility to begin a new life with her somewhere else. Eva is like the Promised Land. He considers going to the bank and telling Fermín that he has found out that Mole is in Brazil and he needs to go there after him. If he can't get any money out of him, he'll at least be able to get him to buy him a ticket. Once there, he'll play it by ear. It's not the most honest idea in the world, but that doesn't worry him too much. He searches through his pockets for Fermín's card, but in vain. He thinks that anyway it's better to go in person. He picks up his pace as he heads to the bank's offices in the centre. Along the way he rehearses his speech. If things work out well, great; if not, God knows what he'll do.

The minute he enters the building, he sees that it's been redecorated. Its previous atmosphere of a postmodern barracks has made way for the aesthetics of an expensive hair salon. The security people, the sheriffs who used to guard the entryway, have metamorphosed into young men wearing blue suits, with refined manners and eternally damp hair. The turnstiles have disappeared. The bank's impressive emblem has been replaced by the image of a sun shining on an ear of wheat wrapped in a banner on which is written "*Banco del Pueblo*", The People's

Bank. Lascano heads straight for the elevators, gets into one with a group of *boludos* – some things haven't changed – and hits the "five" button. When he gets to the fifth floor, he sees there's nothing there. It's empty, the walls stripped bare. Two workers are gathering up their tools.

Hi. Good afternoon. Didn't a bank used to have its offices here? Don't know, could be, we've been clearing everything out because tomorrow another company is moving in. Who hired you? Tepes, the architect. Where can I find him? We're also waiting for him, it's payday.

The elevator opens and a short, stocky and irritable-looking man appears, wetting his fingers as he counts out a thick wad of banknotes. He sees Lascano, stops counting and stares at him. He looks him up and down and immediately understands that he's a cop. He wonders what he wants. Just to be safe, he asks him to wait a second. He pays the workers and dismisses them.

Are you Tepes, the architect? I'm not an architect, superintendent. I'm not a superintendent. So we're in the same boat. Might as well be. Might as well be. How can I help you? Look, I'm trying to find the people from the bank that used to have its offices here. You're out of luck. Why? Don't you read the newspapers? It was taken over by the government; seems they were involved in a lot of monkey business. Then word spread that the bank was about to go under and all the customers made a rush to get their money out. Then what happened? The directors grabbed the dough that was left and took off. You don't say. That's why I always keep my money in cash; you can't even trust the banks in this country.

26

Through the telephone earpiece, Pereyra's secretary's sharp voice informs him that the prosecutor wants to see him right away. The edge in her voice puts him on guard. A few minutes later he is at the door of the courthouse. The line for the elevator is too long and he doesn't want to wait. He climbs up the wide, empty staircase. But on the third flight, which is the first floor, he feels like his heart is about to explode. He sits down to catch his breath. Once he has recovered, he walks across the corridor and presses the elevator button. When it arrives, two very young female lawyers get out, seemingly indifferent to the effect their splendid bodies have on the men that crowd the elevator. On his way down the narrow corridor to the prosecutor's office, Lascano doesn't realize how much he hates this building because at that moment he hates the world, himself, everything. He feels sick, tired and disgusted.

We've got big problems, Lascano. Tell me something I don't already know. I can't seem to get out from under, but you, what do you have to worry about? That this guy is on the loose, for one. What guy? Miranda, who else could I be talking about? A bank robber implicated in the murder of three people has gone scot free, and all because you detained him illegally... Miranda didn't kill anybody. That's not what people around here are saying. I know, but he had nothing to do with the armoured vehicle job. How do you know? Because he told me. And you believe him? I believe him. It was a botched job, the robbers were interrupted by a patrol car that just happened to be driving by, and they took off. The cops took the opportunity to keep the cash. All you have to do is figure out if it was the robbers or the cops who killed the guards. When you've got Chorizo in the mix, anything's possible. Who's Chorizo? A super from the Bonaerense precinct, the one who framed Miranda. Mole isn't a killer, he's a first-rate thief, an intellectual criminal. Doesn't matter, intellectual or not, I want him in jail. What do you suggest we do about it? We? I'm not planning on doing anything; the truth is, I'm sick of all of it, Miranda is your problem now. What do you mean? There's something I've got to do to try to fix my life, just a little, now that I've finally realized I can't change the world. Can I help you? No, it's something I've got to do alone, but I can help you with Miranda. How? If you want to nab Mole, tail his son. Miranda is a family man. Sooner or later the son will lead you to the father. Thanks for the tip, I was starting to think you were in this with him. If you want to know the truth, I'm not telling you this to further the pursuit of justice. Oh no? It's just that I'd rather you get to him before someone like Flores does, someone who'd be capable of doing just about anything to get some money, do you understand? What are you going to do? I need to find someone who left the country, so I'm going to leave. I can get you back on the force, Lascano. You know what, Marcelo, if I did get reinstated, I'd last less time than a fart in a wicker basket. Why? The one who was protecting me was Jorge Turcheli. The chief who died right after he took over? He didn't die, they killed him. The newspapers all said it was a heart attack. Don't believe everything you read. What happened? The Apostles and Turcheli were vying for the job or, rather, there was a struggle between two different ways of seeing the Federal Police as a business opportunity. I don't understand. The Apostles are a group of young officers in bed with cops who deal drugs. And? Turcheli didn't like that; he always said that drugs always come with a lot of violence, and that those narcos don't have any respect for anybody. Turcheli beat them out of the job, so they killed him in his office and made it look like a heart attack. I wouldn't be surprised if the ones who did it had the blessing of some very important politicians. Now the head of the Apostles is sitting in his chair. I have no intention of hanging around to squabble with guys like that…

27

Horacio opens the small door under the grill and sees with satisfaction that the wood fire is burning heartily. Normally he doesn't begin preparing the grill until an hour later, but today is not a normal day. With the money Valli gave him for the job, he'll be able to pay off the last two instalments on the stainless steel grill he had put in two months ago. Outside, a storm is blowing, whistling down the chimney and pushing smoke in his face. This will be the first time he leaves the kid who helps him in charge of the grill. He's been watching him work the last few days, and he trusts he can manage on his own, especially if not a lot of customers show up. He gives him some final instructions, then leaves him to do his job. He drags a bench over to the four-door freezer, reaches up and takes down the package that contains the Ruger he bought from One-Eyed Giardina. He says goodbye and leaves, gets into The Panther, stuffs the package under the seat, drives down the ramp, merges onto the motorway and continues toward Buenos Aires.

It's around noon when he takes the Jujuy exit and parks along Moreno next to a truck depot. He walks through Plaza de Once, crosses the railroad bridge and, zigzagging, reaches the Abasto marketplace, where he

arranged to meet Giardina, who's waiting for him behind
the wheel of an old, beat-up Renault 12.

*You couldn't find more of a wreck, old man? Don't be deceived
by appearances, you have no idea how well it runs. But there
can always be problems. Relax, Horacio, this car you see here
is a fiend. You want a demonstration? The only thing I want
to do is finish this job and return to the grill, so let's get going.
What about the other car? It's already in place.*

They drive in silence. When they reach Agüero, Giardina
points to a parked green Torino. Horacio gets into it;
Giardina drives around the block and double-parks at the
corner. From there he can see Horacio's head through
the rear window.

Horacio prepares himself for the wait. His target, Lascano, should appear on this block, but he doesn't know
when. His worst enemy is sleep. Boredom during indefi-
nite waits can lead to dozing and then the target can get
away. But he came prepared. He looks from side to side,
then in front of him, then in the rearview mirror: apart
from Giardina in the Renault, the street is empty. He
takes a small envelope out of his shirt pocket, opens it
and takes two generous snorts of blow into each nostril,
using the long nail on his baby finger to shovel it in. He
sucks off whatever's left stuck under the nail, then puts
the envelope back in his pocket. He takes the package
out from under his seat, unwraps the gun, checks to make
sure the clip is full, loads a round into the chamber, en-
gages the safety catch and places it between the two front
seats. He waits. There's a walkie-talkie on the passenger

seat so they can alert him to Lascano's approach. But he needs to keep watch because they couldn't guarantee they'd be able to warn him. The problem is impatience, as well as the paranoia the cocaine provokes. He looks through the rearview mirror. Nothing. He saw Lascano only a few times at the station. He never spoke to him, but he remembers him as a bitter and sulky guy. Horacio promised Valli that he knew him well, but now he's not too sure he'll recognize him when he sees him. He remembers he had a peculiar way of walking, as if he had springs on his heels – that'll surely help identify him. The plan is simple. When Lascano walks by the car, he'll get out quietly, walk behind him without him noticing, place the barrel of the Ruger under his ear pointing upward and pull the trigger twice. The advantage of the twenty-two long is that it doesn't make a mess; it's not powerful enough to send the bullet all the way through the skull, so it stays lodged inside the brain, where it's impossible to remove. The victim doesn't fall right away; he staggers a little as if he were drunk, then goes into a coma from which he never awakens. All he's got to do is wait.

Lascano was on the verge of telling that punk kid, prosecutor or not, to go to hell, but he restrained himself. *Anyway,* he thinks, *he's nothing but a kid trying to stay afloat and keep clean in a pond full of shit.* He's sorry he wasn't in the mood to give him some tips on staying alive. Considering the hornets' nests he's sticking that nose into, it's foolhardy the way he's walking around the streets as if nothing would happen to him. He decides to go home on foot. He quickly gets away from the deafening traffic of Tucumán and Uruguay, quickening his pace until he reaches Córdoba. As he passes by the doors of the General Registry Office, the exuberant relatives of a glowing and smiling couple shower him with rice. He shakes the grains off his jacket and out of his hair, reaches the corner and turns toward Callao. The traffic is hellish here, too, but at least the roar dissipates across the breadth of the avenue. He's tired and in a bad mood, and he has no idea where he's going to get the money to fly to Brazil now that he's failed to settle his accounts with the people from the bank. Apparently bankers are better accountants than he is. He decides to go home and see how much cash he has left. It'll probably be enough to get to São Paulo by bus and stay there a few days. From there he'll improvise. A Ford Falcon is parked across the street at the corner of Laprida and Córdoba. The sun reflecting off the windshield makes it so he can't see Onionskin, an ex-cop, or the other two in the car with him. A breeze blows through the street, making a pile of papers dumped in the street swirl into the air. When Lascano can no longer see the Falcon, it drives off, screeching around the corner at full speed. At the next corner it turns toward Fuseli's place and parks a few yards behind the Renault, where Giardina has fallen asleep.

When Horacio sees Lascano walking calmly toward him through the rearview mirror, he recognizes him immediately. He grabs the Ruger and releases the safety catch. He lies down in the passenger seat so Lascano won't see him as he walks by. He curses silently. Because of the direction he's coming from, he'll have to shoot him with his left hand, which he can do, but he feels more confident with his right. He gets out of the car and starts to walk quietly behind him, the Ruger firmly gripped in his left hand. His footsteps are silent and he's lucky the wind is blowing toward him. When he's just three steps away from his target, he raises his gun.

If there's anything that really bothers Lascano, it's the wind in his face. That's why he's grateful when it suddenly changes direction and he feels a gust pushing him from behind. That gust carries to his nose the penetrating scent of barbecued meat that infuses Horacio's clothes. He turns quickly. Fatso is aiming right at his head. He sees the flesh of his finger pressing hard on the trigger. He sees himself dead.

BLAM!

But Horacio is the one who falls. Onionskin, standing next to the kerb, has shot him. The report wakes up One-Eyed Giardina. Startled, he opens his eye and clutches the steering wheel with both hands. Onionskin is pointing his Magnum right between Lascano's eyes. Horacio has landed face down. Blood begins to pour onto the sidewalk. Someone else hits Lascano on the head from behind, knocking him out. Onionskin stashes his gun, takes two steps, pulls a hood over Lascano's head, and the two quickly carry him to the Falcon that just pulled up alongside them. Without moving a muscle, Giardina watches the two men load Perro into the back seat. For a moment, Giardina is too shocked to know what to do. He looks from side to side and behind him and sees that the street is quiet again. He starts the engine and inches backward to where Horacio has fallen. Between the bumpers of two parked cars he sees Horacio bleeding to death. The Ruger he sold him is next to his body. He checks again to make sure there are no witnesses, gets out, dashes over to the gun, picks it up, puts it under his belt, returns to the Renault and takes off.

An hour later, Lascano opens his eyes in the darkness. He's still hooded. He hears a voice.

I think he's awake.

The hood comes off. It's late afternoon and a stream of orange light pours in through the window. It takes a few moments for his eyes to get used to the brightness of the room. He's handcuffed to a chair in a seedy apartment. Across the table, Miranda the Mole's face, grinning at him, comes into focus. Next to him is Onionskin, a merciless psychopath who has the blood of at least five, if not six people on his hands. He's a dimwit who has no business keeping company with Miranda. Everything Lascano had with him is on the table, including Eva's letter and his gun. He's glad it's Miranda and not the Apostles, because then he'd already be dead.

This time I beat you to the punch, Perro. What's up, Mole? As you see, I entertain myself saving your life. Seems like I'm condemned to having my life saved by crooks. You could at least thank me. I thank you, as long as you haven't done it so you can have the pleasure of killing me. That's not my style, as you know very well, Perro. So, to what do I owe the honour? You know. I owed you one. You don't owe me nothing. Not now, but you saved my family when Flores wanted to pull a fast one. I did it for them, not for you. Same difference, Perro. I don't like to owe anybody anything.

In a split second, Miranda's deadpan face lights up with a smile that makes him look ten years younger. He smiles openly, heartily, proudly.

Hey, that was brilliant, you calling the TV station and all. About time TV was useful for something. I can just imagine Flores's face when he saw the huge to-do you stirred up. No, you can't. The cops made him get down on the ground in his thousand-dollar Armani suit. No kidding. Swear to God, when he got up he was so pissed off he was levitating.

Perro and Mole laugh in unison. Onionskin, looking bored and bitter, has no interest in the exchange and sits there staring at his nails.

How did you find out they had a hit out on me? We've all got our sources, Perro, it's a small world. But you really pulled one over on me at the pizzeria, Lascano. Truth is, I've got to admit that you're a master. With that moronic look on your face. Look who's talking. Who do you think you are, Alain Delon? How did you find me? Good detective work, Mole. Cut the crap, who snitched on me? Nobody snitched, I'm telling you, don't go getting paranoid. Truth is you've made yourself a handy bunch of enemies. Who wants to kill you? The dry-cleaner because I didn't pay for my laundry. You never lose your sense of humour. I bet you weren't laughing when I went up in smoke at the station. Don't be so sure, I almost bought a bottle of champagne to celebrate. To tell you the truth, Perro, that was pretty damn stupid of you to leave me at the mercy of Roberti, probably the most corrupt policeman on the force. Believe me, if I'd had any choice, I never would have. I guess not. Is it true you got kicked off the force? I didn't get kicked off, I quit. So why were you after me? You already know. Oh, right, for the dough from the bank. What does a skinflint like you need with money? That's my business. Might it have something to do with this letter written by... Eva? You going to look for her? I told you, that's my business. What are you going to do with me? Nothing. So why did you knock me out? Look, Perro, as long as you're walking around out there, I'm not safe. I need you to disappear. Getting out of where you put me cost a pretty penny. Roberti must be happy. Probably. I also made arrangements for Flores to get lost. Mole, haven't you ever considered that with all your hard work, all the risks you take, in the end the money you steal just goes to making the dirtiest damn cops dirtier and happy? Probably, but that doesn't matter now. What does matter? For you to disappear, Perro. You were a fool. When I offered you money you told me the bank thing was clean. Yeah, and now the bankers have vanished with their clients' money. See what I mean? Will you tell me what the hell you want? I told you, I want you to disappear. Go to Brazil, wherever the hell you want, just get out of Buenos Aires. And if I don't want to? You'll disappear anyway, Onionskin will see to that and if he doesn't, someone else will. I've heard rumours about a group of very heavy-duty officers who want you dead. I don't know what you're talking about. Don't play the fool, Perro, we're all adults here. Today you escaped by the skin of your teeth, but don't push it. I don't want to kill you; you know I don't like the dead. So just make sure you vanish. May I ask you a favour? Under the circumstances, you can ask me whatever you want. Sit here

for ten minutes, okay? Okay. Then, get the fuck out of here,
Perro, do me that favour.

Miranda stands up, smiling. Onionskin picks up Lascano's gun and shoves it under his belt. Then he takes off Lascano's handcuffs. Onionskin and Miranda walk to the door, where another man is waiting. On the other side of the door the elevator doors can be heard, opening and closing. Lascano stands up, barefoot, and walks over to the window. He is on the top floor of a tenement building in Fuerte Apache. He looks out and sees Miranda, Onionskin and two others climb into a Falcon. Just before getting in, Mole look up, waves and smiles. The car takes off and disappears around the corner. Lascano turns and looks around for his shoes, but he doesn't see them anywhere. Then he notices that there's a large envelope on the table along with his things. He picks it up and opens it. Inside is a big wad of dollar bills. He returns to the window. Night is quickly falling. Strange sense of humour Miranda's got, forcing him to walk through that neighbourhood full of muggers and murderers, at night, barefoot, without a peso and with a wad of greenbacks in his pocket. He can't help cracking a short-lived smile. He's going to have to figure out how to get out of there in one piece. If he were a believer he'd cross himself, but since he isn't he touches his testicles and walks out the door.

28

Lascano strolls barefoot up the hill of the Plaza San Martín overlooking Maipú. As he walks he thinks that life, as he has been living it until that moment, has been one great big mistake. He now understands the message from the shadowy person in his dream. He now understands what he needs to change. He realizes that life is actually like a ride on a carousel with no brass ring for the winner. All that crap about austerity, about suffering being more dignified than happiness, that creed about tragedy being nobler than comedy, it's a huge crock of shit, especially for a nonbeliever like himself. All that religion business seems to him like a swindle: *You pay now for a service you'll get only after you're dead.* If you don't expect a reward in the afterlife, what's the point of living like a rat in a sewer during this one?

The men in uniform at the doors of the Plaza Hotel are about to intercept him but, for some reason, they don't dare. A hundred-dollar bill is all the concierge needs to give him a room, even though he has no identification and no luggage. That night he sleeps the sleep of the dead.

In the morning, wrapped in a plush terrycloth bathrobe the hotel provides and wearing slippers decorated with the hotel's insignia, he asks the bellhop to buy him a pair of size forty-two brown loafers at the shoe store on the corner of Marcelo T. de Alvear and San Martín. He orders a superb continental breakfast and, as he savours the freshly squeezed orange juice and contemplates the marvellous view of the treetops in the Plaza San Martín, he feel as if John Lennon were whispering in his ear: *Today is the first day of the rest of your life.*

Miranda the Mole, backed up by Nails and Fathead, spends the whole morning making sure Dandy's house is not under surveillance. They take work in their stride and enjoy a steak sandwich from Argos, on the corner of Lacroze and Alvarez Thomas. To make their wait less tedious, they watch two kids, probably truants from school, playing a game of pool.

Once they're sure the coast is clear, they knock on Dandy's door. Graciela greets them with a smile, a cocktail of three equal parts: relief, joy and reproach. A visit from Mole, when her husband's in the clink, can mean only one thing, and it's something she knows will diminish the tremendous anxiety she has been feeling ever since her husband got arrested. She offers them maté.

How's it going? I don't have to tell you. No, I guess you don't, but I'm really asking how things are going for you. What do I know how things are going for me, the truth is that you men, my dear, I don't know, the life you offer us... But we make you happy every once in a while, don't we? Yeah, the movie's great, but the price of the ticket is way too steep. And the kids? At school. How're they doing? The girl's okay; Raúl has turned out just like his father, no good with the books. He hates it

*and there's no way to get him to sit down and study. My arm
hurts from all the spankings I give him, trying to force him,
but none of it does any good. What can you do, some kids
just don't take to it. I hope he doesn't turn out like his father.
Dandy loves you. Yeah, I know, and what do you want me to
do with that? He's a good man. Hey, if on top of everything
else he was a bad one, you'd have to kill him. You're pissed off?
Well, wouldn't you be? Here we go again, with lawyers and
trials, getting frisked on visiting day, as if I were some kind of
criminal, all so I can watch him rotting in jail. It's no good
for him inside, you know that. Is it for anybody? I guess not.
Don't worry, they're not going to give him much time. Maybe,
but he still has the other sentence to serve. There's almost nothing left on that one, either. Maybe it seems like nothing to you,
but I've spent my whole life waiting for him. I have a favour to
ask of you. What? Give this other envelope to Screw. He needs
it. Mole, you're a good man, too bad you're a crook. What can
I do, nobody's perfect. Take it. Okay, now you can take it easy
and just hang in there. Take good care of the kids and don't
walk out on him, okay? Okay. Don't let him fall apart. You
understand? All right, Mole, all right.*

Along with those last words, Miranda gives her a hug,
dries her tears and runs his hand over her hair. A few
moments later, she's pulled herself together. Miranda
walks to the door, where he gives her a few more pieces
of advice and kisses her on the cheek; she thanks him
and he leaves. Graciela dries her hands on her apron
as a matter of habit, picks up the two envelopes he left
on the table, sighs, opens the little door of the cabinet
where she keeps the good china and sticks them in a
beer pitcher, which plays "Der Liebe Augustin" when

207

she picks it up. Then she goes over to the sink and starts washing the dirty lunch dishes.

That afternoon Lascano tries on an elegant suit of fine Peruvian cotton at Rhoders on Florida Street. He is pleased by his own reflection in the mirror. The trousers need to be shortened. The salesman recommends a tailor a few blocks away who can do it quickly. Lascano rounds out his purchase with underwear, six shirts, a belt, a handkerchief and socks, and requests the lot be sent to the hotel. He takes the trousers with him, and leaves them with a Bolivian tailor who has a tiny shop on Córdoba, under Harrods. He walks to Santa Fe, stops in front of the window of a travel agency filled with magnificent posters of gorgeous landscapes and golden beaches. He enters. A tall and seductive young man greets him with a smile that seems to say that the world is too small for his ambitions. It doesn't take longer than an instant for the young man to figure out how much Lascano's extravagant clothes have cost. He tells himself that this is a serious customer, someone who has come to make a purchase, and he invites him into his office. Effortlessly, and in a matter of minutes, he sells him a ticket to Guarulhos Airport for thirty per cent more than Lascano would have paid anywhere else. A few minutes later, at Rosenthal's, right in front of the plaza, Lascano purchases a small suitcase. He returns to the Galería del Este mall and there, on the first floor, he slips into Susana's Hair Salon, settles into a chair and asks for the full service – cut and shave, with lather and hot towels and, while we're at it, a manicure.

At night, on the corner of Esteban de Luca and Chiclana, there's a truck stop where Doña Elvira makes and serves the best homemade ravioli with pot roast in the entire city, probably the entire country. Generous portions of pasta stuffed with fresh spinach swimming in a sauce as rich and dark as fate itself, accompanied by a tough cut of meat that's been cooked so long and slowly that it melts in your mouth and falls apart with the touch of the fork. That, along with a fresh sharp red wine decanted from a demijohn, is all her regular customers need to rejoice. Held aloft and exuding clouds of a greasy scent that fills the room and sticks to the clothes and hair, plates are passed around piled high with chips, steak and eggs, thick sausage with sauerkraut, braised tripe with beans, meatballs the size of tennis balls, oxtail and potato stew. This is the kingdom of cholesterol with garlic, oil with spices, *tarantella* dessert, wine with soda, and a gastronomic community that never worries about its health or the future and knows how to appreciate the warmth of a calorie-rich entrée in the dead of winter.

Fernando seems quite out of place here with his impeccable attire, his hair cut stylishly and set with gel, and his refined manners. But nobody seems to notice or care, much too busy devouring whatever Doña Elvira's crew sets down on the table in front of them. The young man looks decidedly out of sorts. He realizes that this place, even though it hasn't changed a bit, has nothing in common with his memory of it. He doesn't like the noise and even less the certainty that he will leave there reeking of fried food. By the time he sees his father walk in the door, he's already in a nasty mood. As he walks by the waiter, Miranda orders two plates of ravioli with meat, red wine and soda water.

Hey, son. What's up, Papa? How're you doing? Good, I work a lot and I seem to have less and less free time. What are you doing? The university and politics. Politics? I told you, old man, I've been working for almost two years with the Peronista party. You like politics? Of course I do, why else would I study law? And why's that? Listen, old man, the presidents in this country are either lawyers or in the military, and I don't like the military... But you do want to be President. Well, I wouldn't say no. You can't think of anything better to be? What, like a crook, for instance? Don't get smart with me, and anyway in the end it's almost the same thing. Except politicians are less likely to end up in jail. That's funny. And you, old man, how're you doing? Not bad. What's wrong? They're trying to frame me for a killing that occurred during an attack on an armoured vehicle. I know, but there were three dead. I was giving you a discount because you're my son... Anyway, I had nothing to do with it. There's a cop who's trying to frame me, but since they're also after me for the bank job, I'm not about to start giving explanations. So? Mama doesn't want anything more to do with me. And for good reason. That's true. How do you feel about it? It's a huge blow, but I also know she put up with me for longer than she should have. No argument there. What are your plans? To keep out of sight until things settle down. Seems like a good idea. Really? Truth is that a father like you doesn't help my political career any. Thank you. You're welcome. Well, I have something that will help you. What? Money. Inside this envelope is a number, a code and the telephone number of someone named Christian. Okay. He represents a Swiss bank where I've deposited a lot of money. Keep that information in

*a safe place – or better, memorize it and destroy it. Okay, what
do you want me to do with that money? Use it for whatever
you need. Thanks. Two conditions. I'm listening. That your
mother will never lack anything and that you take care of me if
things don't work out. I'm surprised, old man, that you think
you need to tell me that.*

The waiter brings the drinks and the steaming plates.
Fernando doesn't like that his father has ordered for him
without consulting him. He knows that the rich sauce is
going to disagree with him.

*And the long face? What long face? Yours, who else's? Don't
give me a hard time, old man, don't start on me. Tell me about
yourself, what're you into? Got a girlfriend? No. Forgive me for
asking, but do you even like girls? Back off, old man. It's just
a question. What's wrong with you? You seem so… delicate.
So? So nothing, tell me the truth, are you a faggot? Man, my
generation no longer uses those categories. Do you like men? To
be perfectly honest, up till now I've never come across one who's
turned me on. Does that answer your question? Sort of, though
the "until now" worries me a little. Why? I don't know, you seem
kind of like a sissy, if you want to know the truth. I was raised
by my mother and my aunt. Where the hell were you? Okay,
okay, you got me there, but it's no excuse. Who needs excuses?
Would you feel better if I had a girlfriend? Yes, I would. Okay,
the next time we see each other, I'll bring a friend and introduce
her to you as my girlfriend… It's not a question of making
me feel better. So what is it a question of? Knowing if you're a
real man or not. Does it worry you that much? Yes, it worries
me that much. Look, it's none of your business, and the truth
is you don't have a very open mind on the subject. Speaking*

211

of open... You want to stop insulting me? Oh, so now you're
insulted. I don't have to put up with this shit! Oh no, so what
do you plan to do? Just watch me...

Fernando stands up, does an about-face and walks out.
The door he leaves through swings open and closed and
offers Miranda a scene like something out of a silent
movie: Fernando walking to the kerb, looking one way,
then the other; Fernando raising his arm, opening the
door of the taxi, talking to the driver; the empty street.
He asks for the bill, pays, gulps down the rest of the wine
with soda water, gets up and goes out. There to greet
him at the door are no fewer than six plainclothes cops
with their weapons drawn and pointing at him, three
Falcons and a young man. He raises his hands over his
head. Two of the cops quickly pat him down, handcuff
him and put him in the back seat of one of the cars. It
seems like things haven't worked out.

Lascano takes a taxi to Ezeiza Airport. A few minutes
ago, in perfect synchronicity, Sansone got his passport
to him, issued under the name of Angel Limardi, the
same name that appears on the aeroplane ticket. At the
airport, he checks in and passes through immigration,
then finds out that the flight has been delayed for a couple of hours. He sits down in one of the chairs next to
the window where he can see the runway, the aeroplanes
landing and taking off.

Miranda wakes up in a holding cell in the basement of the
courthouse. He feels really depressed. He already knows
he won't be able to come to any kind of understanding

with this young guy, who turns out to be Prosecutor Pereyra. He's happy he had time to leave the money with his son, so he won't have to depend on anybody else, especially now that he can't rely on Screw any more. He's just started planning his new life in prison when a guard opens the door of the cell and shouts *Miranda!* Mole stands up and approaches him. The guard ushers him out, closes the cell door behind him and accompanies him to the desk in the lobby. Miranda doesn't understand what's going on. The officer on duty takes out the little wooden box where they put all his things and empties it out on the desk. This can only mean one thing: they are releasing him. He suddenly panics. The officer looks at him with derision.

What's up, Miranda, you want to stay?

The fact that they're releasing him at this moment could mean that they're waiting at the door for him – two bullets and into a deep ditch. It wouldn't be the first time this has happened, it's a common scenario for police killers. Miranda picks up his things, stuffs them quickly into his pockets and walks to the door. A policeman accompanies him, then stops a few feet before the door, which another policeman opens. The moment Mole steps onto the sidewalk, full of apprehension, a car drives up and stops. He can't see inside because the windows are tinted. Miranda steps back, ready to try to make a run for it. A window opens. His son Fernando, a big smile on his face, asks him if he wants a ride.

What the hell?... You're free, old man. How did you?... Easy, I forged an immediate release order from the judge assigned to the case. Just like that? Not completely; first I had to find a lawyer who was hungry enough to agree to process the paperwork, knowing that tomorrow they'll drag him in by his ears. How did you find out they had me? When I left that horrible restaurant, I got in a taxi, but I thought I noticed something strange going on. So I got out two blocks away and walked back. When I reached the corner, I saw them arresting you. I guess you weren't that angry at me when you left. I'm still angry but that's got nothing to do with it; what I was most worried about was that they'd put a bullet in your head, so I followed in the taxi. When I saw you enter the courthouse, I relaxed and went to work getting you released. Brilliant kid. Modestly brilliant. Now what do we do? We go someplace where they'll make you a passport, then I take you to Ezeiza. I'll let you know when you can return. Sounds good. I'll get you a first-class lawyer, but there's one condition. Tell me. You're going to stop with the criminal crap, okay? Promise.

29

When Marcelo finds out that Miranda has been released with a forged order, he proceeds to have a temper tantrum that leaves his colleagues in a state of shock. All that shouting and cursing from this usually so well-mannered and composed young man, this epitome of the ideal Argentinean male, echoes through the labyrinths of the Palace of Justice like the fury of a Greek god. Miranda did to Marcelo what he'd done to Lascano, and Marcelo had accused Lascano of being an incompetent. He swears to himself that the guy will not escape him, no matter how clever he is, that he will not rest until he has him handcuffed to the chair that will replace the one he has just kicked to smithereens. When he runs out of steam, he collapses in his armchair and stares at the half-open door as if any moment Miranda the Mole were going to walk right through it. But he doesn't. Instead, his secretary, looking half shocked and half afraid, timidly pops her head in and gently suggests he take the day off. Marcelo feels the urge to leap over the desk, grab her by the scruff of the neck and strangle her, which is a clear indication that he should do as she suggests. He storms out and slams the door behind him. Once outside, he quickly crosses Plaza Lavalle to Libertad. Groups of high school students are lolling about in small groups. The girls remind him of Vanina when he first met her. He must see her. He stops a taxi, collapses into the back seat, closes his eyes and opens the window to let the outside air cool him down.

The university. Libertad, Quintana then El Bajo? Right.

Lascano's arms ache with the tension of holding the aeroplane up for the entire flight. As they descend through the cloud cover, São Paulo begins to take shape through the window. The closer he gets to earth, the better he feels. A river wends its way toward the sea, painstakingly finding a path through the intricate geography of houses, huts and fairytale mansions, clumped together in small neighbourhoods with dead-end streets, other neighbourhoods intersected by highways packed with cars, buses and trucks going every which way, very slowly.

Along the Marginal Highway, right where it borders the Tietê, that stinking black river whose water has the consistency of pudding, the luxurious black Mercedes Benz competes for a foot of space with an old *calhambeque* that's being barely held together with a bunch of wires, a supermodern dump truck and a dilapidated bus crammed full of wary and exhausted workers. The traffic, like the river, stops and goes, and stops and goes. The highway is blocked, there's a detour, it picks up again, then gets cut off again. On one of those detours, the taxi that is carrying Lascano from Guarulhos to Rodoviaria stops in front of an enormous warehouse. Through a gaping hole that looks like a window without glass appears a gigantic papier-mâché *mulatta*, her monstrously huge naked breasts leaning on the sill. The carnival doll's colourful and astonished eyes glue themselves on Lascano like an omen. As the taxi starts moving, he looks at the people in the other cars. Nobody else seems to even notice this enormous sexual demon appearing along the road. Here this colossally erotic woman is simply a part of the landscape. At that moment, Perro wishes he had never quit smoking.

When the taxi stops, he sees her. She's sitting on the front steps of the pavilion of the School of Architecture. Next to her sits Martín, the painter-architect, striking an almost feminine pose as he seduces her with his words. Marcelo can almost imagine what he is saying, and it suddenly crosses his mind that he is not going to stand idly by while that man steals his woman right out from under him. He crosses the street with long, rapid strides. Judging from the surprised expression on Vanina's face and the terrified one on Martín's, his own face must look a lot like that of a rabid lunatic. Marcelo's subsequent actions corroborate this impression. Without saying a word, he grabs the lapels of Martín's studiously casual corduroy jacket, pulls him to his feet and gives him a shove. Martín makes a feeble show of standing up to him, man to man, but Marcelo brings his face to within only a few inches of Martín's and glares at him menacingly. Martín's body exhibits a strange combination of impulses. From the waist down, it wants to hesitate, retreat, it begs to flee. From the waist up, it longs to show courage and defiance. This dichotomy, however, doesn't last long; a planter box full of dead flowers sets the limit of Martín's retreat, even as Marcelo continues to advance upon him. Unable to go back any further, Martín lifts a foot and places it on the edge of the box, striking the pose of a contender, but his upper body is ready to submit and his eyebrows are begging for mercy. His phoniness makes Marcelo laugh, and pity him, but he is determined to humiliate the man. He places his finger on his chest, applies gentle pressure and the architect falls backward over the planter box. As he falls, his head hits a piece of cement, producing an ominous and hollow-sounding noise that makes Marcelo and Vanina stop dead in their tracks. She reacts, bends down over Martín, holds his head and asks him if he is okay. Martín opens his eyes, lifts up his head and says yes. Marcelo turns and walks away the way he came. For the first time in his life he feels the intense satisfaction of having done something very, very wrong. He is certain that he has also ruined any chance he may have had to win Vanina back. He's one of those people who believes that women always side with the weak. That's why he's surprised when she catches up with him, grabs his arm and forces him to turn and face her; then she asks him if he is crazy. They engage in a discussion that ends up in the Etcetera – a hotel you pay for by the hour on Monroe Street, near Figueroa Alcorta, one with a splendid view of the edge of the Palermo forest. There, in the serene glow of sexual gratification, as they contemplate their magnificent naked selves in the mirror on the ceiling, Marcelo proposes to her. Vanina says yes, without missing a beat, and curls up against his body. The boy thinks about how happy his mother and mother-in-law are going to be when she tells them, then experiences a moment of distress: he has the sensation that his life is starting to turn into an eternal Sunday afternoon.

By the time Lascano reaches Juquehy, it's already dark. The only place he can find to stay for the night is a tourist hotel built right in the middle of the *mato*. The rooms, rustically elegant, are far apart and surrounded by bromeliads and orchids. The town is very small. He eats dinner at the hotel, takes a shower and stretches out on the bed. He falls into a deep sleep, as if he'd been punched in his lower jaw, and wakes the next morning as if he'd dropped off two minutes earlier. Along the dusty streets of Juquehy, his white suit makes him look like a wealthy landowner or a *pai de santos* out for a stroll, and the locals look at him with a kind of reverence. He asks directions and finds his way to Rua Lontra. It is a dirt road gutted by rain. The further he walks along it, the steeper and more gutted it becomes and the vegetation along the sides grows denser. As he comes around a curve he sees a pond fed by the tiny bubbling *cachoeira*. Just beyond it he sees three houses. None has numbers or any distinguishing marks. They look deserted. He knocks on the metal door of the first one; nobody answers. The door to the second is blocked by a gate. He presses the doorbell and a spine-tingling mastiff, as quiet as a shadow, appears and begins to pace eagerly back and forth in front of him, never taking his eyes off him. He seems eager to plunge his fangs into this piece of meat that might dare enter his territory. The third, perched at the top of the slope, has a small wooden door in front of a log staircase that leads to a terrace, where a hammock is hanging and, behind that, some blue latticework. There's

219

no doorbell, so he claps his hands, but the only person who seems to hear him is a man coming down the hill carrying a bicycle on his shoulder.

I'm looking for a woman named Eva, do you know her? The man smiles widely and points to the house in front. *Ah, sim. Senhora Eva. Do you know where I can find her?* He scratches his head and gazes at Lascano with empty eyes. *Where is she? Dónde está? Na praia. In the beach? Sim, na praia, barraquinha. Barraquinha?* The Brazilian mimes drinking. Lascano imitates him. *A bar on the beach?* The man smiles and gestures for Perro to follow him.

Lascano discovers that going down is more difficult and dangerous than going up. The man he is following is a thin, sinewy mulatto whose feet know every single stone and obstacle, every crack along the way. Perro decides to step precisely where the man steps. When he reaches the street that borders the sea, the man gets on his bicycle and starts riding away. Lascano watches him leave without turning to look back. Lascano continues in the same direction. The man said there would be something orange. He said "they will be there", or did he misunderstand? Lascano's heart tightens when he considers the possibility that Eva is involved with someone. He needs to find out. He doesn't know what he will do if that is the case. He doesn't even know if he will approach her. He doesn't want his appearance to cause any trouble for her, doesn't want his life, which now has nothing to do with her, to upset whatever life she has managed to build. Eva, however, is the only thing he can see in his own future. Without her the world seems barren, useless, senseless. He is afraid of what he will find, but he continues on the tail of one specific memory.

After walking for ten minutes along that street paved with octagonal concrete tiles, he sees the mulatto about thirty yards ahead, standing next to his bicycle and pointing to the beach. When Lascano waves back to show that he sees, the man gets back on his bike and continues on his way. To Lascano's right, between two houses, there's a passageway at the end of which he can see the sea. He starts down it. It comes out a little above a terrace with orange-coloured umbrellas. Just as he's about to take a step in that direction, he hears a familiar voice calling "Victoria". A child appears, running toward the terrace. The little girl is laughing and carrying a black rag doll wearing a polka-dot dress. Eva appears right behind her. Her hair is loose, she's very tanned and she's wearing a bikini top and a beach towel on which multicoloured dragons, enlivened by her stride, are engaged in battle. Lascano has the same impression he had when he first saw her. The same feeling. The same agitation. The same sense of unreality. How to approach her? How to greet her? What words to use? What gestures, now that all he feels is the desire to shout and cry and die?... Just then a man appears on the terrace behind her and starts to walk toward her. The child jumps into his arms, he hugs her and presses her against his chest. The girl looks in Lascano's direction. Again, those familiar eyes that seem to swirl as they stare at you. Eva's eyes, her mother's eyes, little Juan's eyes and now Victoria's eyes. The man comes up to Eva, takes her by the waist; she turns around slightly and kisses him on the lips. She is glowing, she looks happy and beautiful, but when

221

the man turns around Lascano feels like he's been struck by lightning: it is his friend Fuseli. He feels his knees weaken and buckle under him until he finds himself sitting on the stair at the end of the path and the beginning of the sand, the same sand over which Eva, Fuseli and little Victoria walk serenely toward the water. Behind them the sea lazily licks the shore; further out, the jungle islet fills with birds. His head is spinning; he feels as if he's on the verge of passing out. The last thing he wants is to meet them in this state. He wants to be thousands of miles away, he wants to take off running, he feels he's about to burst. He stands up, staggers back up the passageway to the street, where the sun is dazzling. A man is standing right there in front of him. He shields his eyes from the sun with his hand and recognizes him: it's Miranda the Mole.

That's all I needed. What the hell are you doing here? I came to find you. Me? I had to split; problems with a little prosecutor who had it in for me. And your family? Very well, thank you. The boy is all grown up and Duchess has had enough of me. No, really, can you please tell me what the hell you are doing in this place? Look, I had to decide from one minute to the next where to go, and this was the only place in the world where I knew somebody outside of Buenos Aires. You're nuts. Look who's talking. What are your plans? No idea. You? Me, neither. Didn't work out with the girl you came to find, eh? How do you know? Come on Perro, you think you're the only one who can make deductions? Look at your face. There's another guy? I'd rather not talk about it. We don't have to... And what about that story you told me about taking your grandson out for a walk, eh? That's something I'd rather not talk about. We don't have to...

As if obeying some kind of tacit agreement, Lascano and Miranda start walking up the street. Mole looks at the octagonal paving stones; Perro looks at the sea.

You going to tell me who snitched on me when you nabbed me at the pizzeria? You still on about that? Damn right. Nobody snitched, Mole, it was pure luck. Really? Don't you know that you crooks are always unlucky?…

…Hey, they say up north is the place to be. Where to? Bahia? That's all I need, to end up going to Bahia with this guy. What did you say? Nothing, don't pay any attention to me. So, want to go? Whatever, I'm so fucked I don't know whether to shit or go blind. Listen, I heard there are some banks in Salvador that are a piece of cake. Don't start with that crap, Miranda, I'm not going to rob a bank with you. No, of course, not now, not when we're loaded, but this dough isn't going to last forever…

On the beach, Eva and Victoria are building a sandcastle. Fuseli lights a Tuscan cigar, turns, and looks down the alleyway leading to the street. A few minutes earlier he thought he saw a familiar figure, but then he decides it's just his nostalgia playing tricks on him.

A few yards away, Lascano and Miranda keep arguing as they climb back up the hill.

NEEDLE IN A HAYSTACK

Ernesto Mallo

Superintendent Lascano is a detective working under the shadow of military rule in Buenos Aires in the late 1970s. Sent to investigate a double murder, he arrives at the crime scene to find three bodies. Two are clearly the work of the Junta's death squads, murders he is forced to ignore; the other one seems different.

The trail leads Lascano through a decadent Argentina, a country poisoned to its core by the tyranny of the regime. The third corpse turns out to be that of Biterman, money lender and Auschwitz survivor who has recently called on the debts of the well-born Amancio. When Lascano digs too deep, he must confront Giribaldi, an army major, quick to help old friends, but ruthless in dealing with dissenters, such as Eva, the young militant with whom Lascano is falling in love. An honest cop in a police state, Lascano goes in search of the truth in a land where honesty can mean risking your life.

PRAISE FOR *NEEDLE IN A HAYSTACK*

£8.99/$14.95
CRIME PAPERBACK ORIGINAL
ISBN 978–1904738–56–5
www.bitterlemonpress.com